GREEN FLASH

at SUNSET

Marcia Capo

*To Mary —
with heartfelt
wishes for good
health and
happiness —
marcia*

Green Flash at Sunset Copyright 2016, Marcia Capo. All rights reserved.

No part of this book maybe produced in any form or by any means, or stored in a database or retrieval system without prior written permission from the publisher, except in the case of brief quotations embodied in critical articles or reviews. Making copies of any part of this book for any purpose other than your own personal use is a violation of the United Stated copyright laws. Entering any of the contents into a computer for mailing list or database purposes is strictly prohibited unless written authorization is obtained from the owner.

E-mail: gammiecapo@gmail.com

To Robert, Dan
And Cristina

1

The day the invitation arrived, the one that would change Phillip Ashcroft's life, the weather could not be described in terms as basic as hot and humid. No, brutal was more like it for the heat, oppressive to the point of suffocating for the humidity. If you were a walker, you had to do it at the break of dawn on such a day. Wait an hour, and just the short trip to the mailbox would have you wondering whether or not you could make it back. That was exactly why he had stopped for the mail on his way in from shopping at Publix this morning. Anything to keep from going back out into this sweltering sauna.

As he approached the door, the thought occurred to him that you could almost regret having moved here after roasting your ass off for what was it, five straight months now? Only almost, though, because when you stopped to consider that in the coming months back in Michigan you would freeze off the same part of your anatomy, you might change your mind. Still, this was October, for God's sake, and by now you should be entitled to some small measure of relief even here on the southwest coast of Florida. It wasn't coming today, though, that was for damn sure. There wasn't even one lone breeze from the Gulf to nudge the palm fronds. Days like this brought a nostalgic memory of October in Michigan, the air so clear and cool and delicious to breathe, he used to think it should be bottled.

Savoring the rush of the other kind of cool air that greeted him as he stepped into the condo balancing two bags of groceries and a stack of mail, he uttered the words that sprang to his lips often in this kind of weather: "Thank you, Willis Carrier," invoking the name of the man responsible for the gift of air conditioning. Yes, it truly was a gift, he'd decided long ago, and a major one at that. He said it frequently, fervently and out loud, just the way he had when Claudia was alive. How, he wondered, had people ever survived here without that life-saving invention?

He set the mail on the counter and began placing the perishables in the refrigerator. Orange juice and milk on the top shelf, cheese and deli meat in the snack drawer, bagged salad and a cucumber in the vegetable bin. Not for the first time, handling the long green cylinder made him wonder why he still bought them when truth be told, he didn't like them. Never had. He remembered his father and older brother Gordon eating cucumbers fresh from the vegetable garden when he was a boy. His mother would bring them in, rinse off the rich Michigan soil, and they would eat them out of hand, passing the salt shaker between them. But he never ate them, not until he married Claudia. She loved them, adding thin slices into salads, and he ate them to please her. But now, two years since that terrible day he lost her, he was still putting them in the cart when he went shopping. Force of habit, that's all it was. Usually they ended up half eaten, the rest tossed into the garbage grinder. Sighing, he opened the pantry door and put three cans of soup, a box of rice and a package of candy bars on a partially filled shelf. Claudia used to tease him about his sweet tooth and the way he always had to have a stash of his childhood favorite on hand. Milk chocolate Hershey bars with almonds, his very own comfort food.

That done, he brought the recycle bin from the laundry room before pulling out one of the white wicker chairs. He tried to ignore the funny snap in his left knee as he sat, something that had started up recently. Not all that recent was the stiffness in his joints when he got out of bed in the morning. That had been going on for the last couple of years. Well hell, he was no youngster. A half year from now he'd turn sixty-eight, and then there would be just one more birthday before the big seven-oh. Things were bound to start wearing out as you approached that stage in life, weren't they?

As expected, at first glance the mail looked like the same old collection of junk except for the phone bill which he set aside. He began dumping the rest into the bin, taking a quick second look as it fell. Ads, announcements of yet more doctors and dentists opening practices, probably eager to settle here ahead of retirement. An invitation to a financial seminar offering a choice of a free lunch or dinner made him shake his head. Free? Who in his right mind wanted to eat bland, tasteless food at ridiculously early mealtimes and yes, pay for it sitting through endless, boring sales pitches? Into the bin with that one.

There was another one of those two-for-one cruise offers that had sent arrows into his heart for a long time after Claudia died. She'd mentioned on more than one occasion how nice it would be to go on a cruise, and he always responded with his usual cavalier assurance that there was plenty of time for such pleasures. She used to tease him about that, telling him his nickname should be "Mister One of These Days" but he felt he had good reason for postponing such adventures. Enjoy settling into the welcome ambience of the subtropics was his theory, and wait a few years for it to become old hat. There would be plenty of time later to scratch the itch for something new, a change of scene. Their recent move was still enough of a novel experience as far as he was concerned. They were relatively young and healthy, after all, with a good spread of years ahead of them. Who could have foreseen her being struck down so soon, so tragically, so completely unexpectedly?

 He was almost finished with the dumping when he spotted it. Hold on, what was that falling from where it had been stuck between two oversized pizza ads? He retrieved a small yellow envelope, the only other piece of mail addressed to Phillip Ashcroft without "or current occupant" next to it. And wonder of wonders, he saw that it was written, not typed, and in honest-to-God old-fashioned handwriting. Very nice handwriting, in fact, and it had a feminine aspect to his eye. The envelope looked to be about the size of the ones invitations came in. Turning it over, he saw the return address was on Bayview Way, a complex of mid-rise buildings with ground-floor garages and spacious storage units. It was the newest, priciest and final stage of development here in Banyan Bay and he remembered walking through the models right after they were finished last year. Eye-popping beautiful, they offered three bedrooms, two baths, and a powder room just off the marble entry. Fireplaces too, in the penthouses. The view from each balcony was breathtaking, sweeping over mangroves to the bay, the Key and the Gulf beyond. He thought about Claudia and how she would have loved one of those units, yet never would have told him. Some women might, but not his Claudia, who from the very beginning always made sure he understood she was more than happy with the lifestyle he was able to provide.

He opened the envelope and sure enough it was an invitation, a witty cartoon-style drawing of a bunch of people yakking and holding cocktail glasses. Someone named Karla Lynne Anderson requested his presence at a cocktail party at her place a week from this coming Friday at 5:30 p.m. There was a phone number with the standard "regrets only" below it, and "Casual dress" scrawled below that. Well, what else would make any sense in this damned heat? Although, who knew, by then the weather might have turned more normal and cooled down a little.

He'd have to think about it. After Claudia died, some of the neighbors asked him to cocktail and dinner parties, usually by phone or bumping into him on the street when he was out walking. At first he accepted their kind gestures. It was hard going without her, but he made himself do it. After a while though, he started finding excuses to decline the invitations, and pretty soon they stopped coming. Truth was, he felt uncomfortable being the lone man among all the couples and though he appreciated their thoughtfulness, he was not at ease in the role of the man people feel sorry for. It would have been different back home in Pine Ridge with friends he and Claudia had known forever, but here in Banyan Bay he felt an awkwardness in social situations, a feeling of incompleteness without her at his side. Damn it, she wasn't supposed to die just two years into what should have been a long span of them, enjoying the retirement they'd looked forward to so eagerly. And even though he'd given himself points for coming to terms with the anger and resentment all the so-called experts claimed were part of the grieving process, none of that did a thing for the loneliness, the emptiness that pervaded every corner of the condo. He missed her so much, missed her vitality, her voice, her laugh, her very Claudia-ness. He'd always loved going to parties with her, proud of the way she attracted people at those affairs, and then sharing observations about the other guests afterwards. Now, going without her only served to cruelly emphasize the loss of all that. But come to think of it, it had been a while since he'd gotten an invitation. This woman had to be a newcomer to the Bay and she must be single, having sent the invitation in her name only. Maybe he wasn't the only lone person around here, and maybe he ought to stop dwelling on it and quit worrying about people feeling sorry for him. He'd have to give this invitation some thought and not just automatically respond with regrets.

He was hungry and realized it was past time for lunch. He made a pastrami sandwich and poured beer into a tall glass, thinking about how he used to drink it right from the bottle when he was young. Claudia's influence, of course. Beer should be drunk from a classic Pilsner glass, she insisted, or a traditional mug, preferably copper or pewter. And she swore wine tasted better when sipped from the fine crystal stemware she enjoyed buying. The auto parts business was booming then, and Phillip was reaping increasingly lucrative commissions and bonuses. Claudia had retired, a bit reluctantly, and became deeply involved in community activities. They had adjusted to a life without the children they'd hoped for, and as time went on and money became more plentiful, they allowed themselves certain indulgences. Occasional travel was one of them, and their interest in wine began on a tour that included California's magnificent wine country and a memorable dinner excursion on the wine train in Napa. Phillip developed an affinity for the grape and the more he learned about its intricate journey from vine to shelf, the more finely honed his taste became. But beer was perfect for today and it tasted great, cold and refreshing as it slid down his dry throat.

After a while he noticed the sun had started to lower and the palm fronds were moving, stirred by a sudden stiff westerly breeze blowing in from the Gulf. He decided to finish his beer on the deck, and was pleased to find it was considerably cooler now. He watched a mother duck swiftly steering her babies away from under the baleful eye of a Great Blue heron on the bank, and silently cheered. Then a snowy white egret swooped down, plunged into the water and flew off with a fish wiggling in its beak, gleaming silver in the sun's slanting rays. Phillip loved watching the wildlife, and would always remember being just yards away from a sleek bobcat one early evening shortly after they'd moved in. The creature sat staring at him for a long moment before it rose gracefully and disappeared into the nature preserve bordering the lake. Beautiful, and a thrill he never forgot.

He finished the beer and sat for a while longer listening to the splashing of the fountain and thinking about the invitation. He decided, finally, that he would go. It was time to quit this dithering, time to stop feeling self-conscious. What did he have to lose? He'd put on a nice pair of khakis and make a selection from the stack of shirts Claudia bought for him because she couldn't resist the fabulous bargains she kept finding at the malls. Most of them still had tags attached because he'd never gotten around to wearing them. Well, time to break them out. He could almost hear Claudia urging him to stop this foolishness, get out there and join the living while he was lucky enough to be one of them.

2

He recognized the place as soon as he got off the elevator on the fifth floor and saw the open door down the corridor. It was one of the three models he'd walked through that day. Approaching, he heard laughter and people talking loudly over the music. Phillip hesitated at the door and almost immediately, a blonde woman walked up to him and offered her hand.

"Hi, Phillip. Karla Anderson. We haven't met, but Marnie Davis told me who you were a couple of weeks ago. We were having coffee on her front porch when you walked by." Her hand felt soft but the handshake was firm.

"Nice to meet you, Karla. Thanks for inviting me."

"So glad you could make it." She had a very engaging smile. Now that he thought about it, she looked familiar. It came to him that he'd seen her from a distance around the racquet club, always dressed in tennis outfits. Up close, he saw she had a pretty face, tanned just enough to enhance her blue eyes. Still holding his hand, she led him into the living room, pointing out Marnie and Ted Davis, who were talking to a group of people in the middle of the crowded room. Both waved as he walked past. She guided him toward the bar at the far corner of the room, next to the sliding doors that opened on to the balcony.

"Of course you know Kevin Whitfield," she said, and the handsome young blonde man behind the bar leaned forward to shake Phillip's hand, grinning. Phillip smiled back at the popular tennis pro who ran the racquet club.

"Great to see you, Phillip. I was beginning to think the only time I'd get to see you is at the monthly meetings." Turning to Karla, he said "I'm sure you know this guy is in charge of running the place!"

"Come on, Kevin, you're forgetting about the dozens of times a day I pop in to interrupt you with some question or other."

Karla had forgotten that Phillip was the president of the Banyan Bay management association. She had read it in the handbook she'd gotten when she moved in but didn't make the connection when Marnie mentioned his name and told her he lived just down the street. She had never attended a monthly board meeting and now made a mental note to make sure she wouldn't miss any in the future.

"I'll see you in a few minutes, Phillip," she said, adding "I'm leaving you in good hands. He's not only the best tennis coach I've ever run into, but he has a reputation as a great moonlighting bartender and I feel lucky snagging him for tonight. I hear his specialty is the time-honored Manhattan. That was my Dad's favorite drink, and somehow you look like a man who might also be a devotee."

"She's right, you know," he said to Kevin, watching her cross the room. "As it happens, a well-made Manhattan is my favorite, and I make one for myself every night. She must be a mind reader. Skip the cherries, though."

"Nice lady. Excellent tennis player, too. She picks up everything I teach her faster than anyone else."

"I've seen her around the club, but this is the first time I've met her. Very kind of her to invite me to the party tonight."

He walked toward the open doors to the balcony, musing about her comment. Had she guessed his preference for a Manhattan because she'd classified him as an older man? Not in her father's age range, certainly, but maybe not all that far off either. Which was fine with him, and in fact he found it amusing.

Standing at the railing, he was oblivious of the chatter around him. The view really was spectacular. The last rays of sunlight flashed on the ripples as boats sped by on the bay, their wakes creating a field of moving diamonds. Knowing the best was yet to come, he stood watching until the sun started to sink into the Gulf, turning the scattered clouds into streaming banners of pink and purple and gold.

He was so entranced, he hadn't noticed that his hostess was at his side until she spoke in a soft voice.

"Beautiful, isn't it? I never get tired of doing exactly what you're doing, standing perfectly still, looking and looking till the show is over."

He nodded, and she touched his arm, looking at his glass. "I see you're almost ready for a refill. Let me get it."

The next few hours passed quickly as Phillip chatted with people, a few new arrivals and others he recognized as snowbirds returning for the season. Karla was a superb hostess, covering the large living room and lanai, making sure everyone was offered drinks and tasty selections from the platters of hors d'oeuvres. She had engaged the services of a delightful young woman named Laura who Phillip remembered from some of the parties at the club and at the homes of neighbors. As he helped himself to a particular favorite, a couple of mushrooms stuffed with lobster and spinach, she told him she had missed him lately and was glad to see him tonight. Her comment deepened the warmth he was feeling. Yes, he was indeed glad he'd accepted the invitation.

It was full dark when he saw that the room was thinning out and decided it was time to leave. He waited till she was alone, then walked over to say goodnight.

"Thank you for a great evening, Karla. I had a wonderful time and I'm so glad you invited me." His words and delivery sounded stiff to his own ears, much like a schoolboy thanking a classmate after a birthday party, but her smile was warm as she slid her hand into his and tightened her grip ever so slightly.

"I'm glad too, Phillip." She seemed about to say more, but just then another couple came to say goodnight. He stood there for a few minutes but it looked as if the chat could go on for a while, so he left.

Walking home, Phillip thought about the feeling he'd gotten each time she took his hand in hers. He could still feel it, a sensation like some kind of low-voltage current. Karla Anderson was a lovely woman and she'd made him feel at ease from the minute she welcomed him at the door. How could he have hesitated about accepting the invitation? Everything about the party was delightful, his hostess most of all. He found the other guests, those he knew and those he met for the first time, friendly and interesting to chat with. Then there were those delectable appetizers. He'd eaten quite a few and knew some cheese and crackers would suffice for dinner later.

He was almost home, ready to cross the street, when he spotted the redhead, the woman he'd seen often on his early morning walks the last few weeks. She appeared fairly young, maybe early forties. He could barely make her out in the dim light from the lamp post on the corner, but he knew her by her brisk stride and the outline of her pony tail. She was an odd one. He had smiled and waved at her once, but there hadn't been a response, so he understood that her focus was strictly on listening to whatever she was hearing through her earphones. He and Claudia had disdained them, preferring to listen to bird calls and the rustle of banyan trees shaken by the wind. This woman certainly was different from the other people he met who were walking, running, cycling, or gliding by on in-line skates. They almost always smiled or called out a friendly "Hi!" and sometimes the walkers stopped to exchange a few words about the weather. But not this one. He'd gotten a good look at her whenever she strode toward him from the opposite direction and she struck him as a pretty woman, at least the part of her face that wasn't hidden behind gigantic sunglasses. She always wore shorts and a tank top, and that pony tail swung rhythmically with each step. She walked alone, and he mused about her sometimes, but really she was none of his business.

Phillip had made a slight change in his usual three-mile walking route. Although he liked alternating the pattern every now and then, he did not normally include Bayview Way and the adjoining streets closer to the water. They offered only peeks of the bay between each cluster of buildings, while the nature trail was by far the most scenic portion of his walk. A small white gazebo at the very end was a splendid destination for pure enjoyment of the sights and sounds and smells of the water. It was a fine place for fishing and boat-watching, and afforded a clear view of the Key.

But now it was different. Starting the morning after the party, he'd expanded his route to include Karla's street, hoping to run into her. This was new for him, even thinking about a woman, much less anticipating seeing her, something that hadn't happened since Claudia died. But Karla Lynne Anderson seemed to have invaded his brain and gotten stuck there. He kept seeing her face and remembering that little jolt of electricity each time she'd put her hand in his. And today, as he walked past her building, he came to a decision. He would call her and ask her for a dinner date. She wasn't going to give him any peace, so he'd better just do it. What was the worst that could come of asking her? She could decline, and if she did he suspected she would handle it graciously. Of course he would be disappointed, but at least he would have given it a shot. And if he suggested another time and she demurred, it would mean she wasn't interested. It would not be the end of the world, and he'd accept it. Okay, now that was settled. He would call her today. Satisfied, he picked up his pace and headed back to Banyan Bay Boulevard to finish his walk.

It was almost dusk when he picked up the phone and dialed her number, looking at the invitation that was still on the glass top of the wicker table. When she answered the phone and he identified himself, the warmth in her voice sent little ripples of pleasure through him.

"Phillip! I was just thinking about you. Sorry we didn't get more of a chance to chat when you were leaving the other night."

"You were busy. I think everyone at the party was eager to tell you how much they enjoyed it. It was great, and you were very nice to include me."

"My pleasure."

Short pause. Go ahead, ask her. He cleared his throat.

"I was wondering, Karla, if you might happen to be free to have dinner with me either on Friday or Saturday, whichever evening would work best for you."

"What a nice offer. Saturday sounds perfect."

So far, so good. How long had it been since he asked a woman for a date? Never mind, she had made it easy and he was smiling when he hung up.

3

The waiter poured a small amount of the wine, a Chenin Blanc from a small winery in Sonoma, and waited as Phillip swirled it gently and tasted it, letting it linger on his tongue before nodding approval. When the glasses were filled, Karla proposed a toast.

"To the good life here in paradise!"

"Which keeps getting better," he added, and she smiled as they drank.

"You are quite the wine expert, Phillip. This is absolutely delicious."

"Thank you. I am far from being an expert, but I began a love affair with the grape years ago when my late wife Claudia and I toured the wine country in northern California."

"That part of the country is on my bucket list of places I simply have to visit. It must be heaven."

They sat quietly for a few moments sipping the wine. Then Karla said "I really like this place. I haven't been here before, but I remember reading a review in the paper and thinking what a great name that is for a seafood restaurant. Something's Fishy. It intrigued me. I have to admit I'm a sucker for names like that, the cornier the better, actually. I have my hair done here at a place called A Cut Above. Booked my first appointment because I liked the name, and luckily I'm very pleased with the stylist. I've gone to her ever since."

"Okay, then I have to admit I had my hair cut back in Michigan at a place called the Hair Port, believe it or not. Corny enough for you? So that makes two of us."

They were laughing when the waiter returned to take their order and refill their glasses. Here he was on an actual date and he was feeling relaxed, the little bit of nervousness he'd felt when he picked her up gone. Over dinner, they compared backgrounds.

"So you came here from Michigan, Phillip? Where, exactly?"

"A small city in the western part of the state, Pine Ridge. How about you? I think I detect a good old Midwestern accent. Am I right?"

"Yes, Indiana. South Bend, to be precise. But my father was born and raised in the upper peninsula of Michigan. Did you know people up there are known as Yoopers?"

Phillip laughed. "Yes, I do know, and they're proud of it. I've been there a few times on fishing trips. I also had a couple of customers up there, and I always enjoyed calling on them. In summer, mostly, and late spring and early fall. Not so much in the winter months. It's desolate in some places, but wild and beautiful. How did he happen to end up in Indiana?"

"Jobs, or I should say, lack of them in the U.P. My Dad's best friend from high school moved to South Bend and settled there. He convinced Big Karl to come down because there was a lot of construction going on and workers were making more money than anyone back home ever dreamed of. He was young and strong and liked the idea. He told me once that he used to get pretty homesick for the far north, but he never moved back because he fell in love with an Indiana girl. He married my Mom, Linnea, and they had two girls, my sister June and me. I was the son he didn't have, I guess, because not only did I have Big Karl's name, but I was good at sports and he came to as many of my softball and basketball games as he could manage. June was the girly one, and I got more that way as I grew up, so he had to miss the thrill of my being a star college athlete. As if that would have happened. But he loved me and encouraged me to be whatever I wanted to be. I still miss him and I always will. I loved my mother just as much but there was this special bond between my father and me."

"And he liked his Manhattans, right? I wondered, when you mentioned that at your party, if I reminded you of him in some way."

She laughed. "Yes, there is something about you that made me think of him, but if you're hinting that I had tagged you as being in his age group, forget it. Not even close. I guess I mention him a lot because he was the big man in my life. Anyway, Phillip, I don't think you're all that much older than I am."

"Okay, full disclosure right now. I'll be turning sixty-eight on my next birthday, and I know you can't be...well, I'm not good at guessing ages, especially women's..."

"Stop, I'll save you. I never have a problem telling people my age. I turned fifty-six this past summer. Not all that much difference. Eleven years, for Pete's sake. And besides, you look a lot younger."

"And so do you. Much, much younger. I'm not saying that just to return your compliment. I would have pegged you at about ten years younger, at least."

It was true. She was tall, slim but curvy, and he found her beautiful to look at as she sat across from him. She was wearing a light blue dress that matched perfectly the color of her eyes, and a crystal necklace that sparkled in the light from the candle on the table. He was finding it difficult to keep his eyes from straying to the lovely cleavage that showed just above the soft folds of the draped neckline.

They exchanged brief histories of their marriages and discovered they had unintentional childlessness in common. Phillip spoke first, looking more than a little sad.

"Claudia and I never gave a thought to the possibility of problems when it came to having children. You got married, waited perhaps a year or so to settle into just being husband and wife, then you started a family. That's how it was with our friends, anyway. But as it turned out, there were problems. God knows we tried. Different doctors, lots of tests and medications, thermometer readings to determine cycles, that sort of thing. But in spite of all our efforts, it didn't work. Of course that was decades ago. The field of fertility research back then was nowhere close to what it is today."

Karla made a sympathetic sound, and he continued, twirling the stem of his wine glass. "We did, of course, talk about adoption, but kept putting it off. Claudia liked her job and she was good at it. She got raises regularly, and it was the same with me. It was a boom time for the auto parts industry, and the money kept rolling in. Life was good and we were more than comfortable financially. A lawsuit concerning Claudia's parents' fatal auto accident was finally resolved and she received an enormous settlement as a result. As time passed, I guess we got used to our status, I mean being just the two of us, and we were content with the way things were going. You might say we were coasting and bottom line, we never got around to actually following through with the business of adopting. We did look into it after the first five years or so of marriage, even went so far as to send for an application form to an out-of-state private adoption agency. We filled it out, and beyond that I honestly don't remember what happened. I guess we must have dropped the ball along the way somehow, not following up…"

He let the thought trail, sighed and continued. "But I'd be lying if I told you I haven't regretted letting that opportunity slip by, however it happened. I've thought so many times how nice it would be to have a family, and I have to confess to being envious of friends who have children and grandchildren. Especially at Christmas, when I get cards with photos of all those beautiful, beaming little faces."

"I know exactly what you mean. For me, for Caleb and me, getting pregnant wasn't the problem. In fact, that was exactly the reason we got married." She took a sip of the coffee the waiter had just brought before relating her story.

She and Caleb had been together since senior year in high school and were married six months before graduating from Indiana University. It was what people back then called a shotgun wedding, but as it turned out it was unnecessary because she miscarried a month later. Still, they were in love and the next ten years were relatively happy except for the repeated miscarriages. The stress from those, she felt, must have played a major role in the gradual erosion of the marriage. Time after time, hope and joyful anticipation followed by painful loss eventually took its toll. A new restlessness seemed to take hold of Caleb, and slowly but surely she began to feel they were living more like roommates than spouses. So when he broached the subject of divorce after dinner one evening, it wasn't exactly a shock.

"Just like that, out of the blue, without any warning? I would guess there must have been another woman in the picture. Was there?"

"Yes, there was another woman. I can't say it was out of the blue, exactly, because the classic signs were there. Coming home late, last-minute business trips, mysterious phone calls, you know, sudden hang-ups when I answered. Stupid me, I didn't put it all together, and I realized later it was because I didn't want to believe it. I was in denial and incredibly naive. My God, Phillip, there was even the perfume on the suit jacket thing! A cheap scent, one I never would wear. Sorry if that sounds snobbish. Cyndi was new in the office, young, pretty, divorced, crying on his big comforting shoulder. He was ripe for playing the understanding counselor, couch included. Could it get any more life-imitates-soap opera than that?"

"There have been events in my life that I swear could be categorized as jumping right off the scripts of soap operas." He permitted himself a rueful smile. "Was she a passing fancy or did he marry her?"

"Oh, he married her. She was pregnant, you see. History repeating itself but it turned out a lot differently. Caleb got to be a proud father." She shook her head and added with a bitter smile, "And to complete the fairy tale, she had twin girls. I have to say they were adorable. I used to see them in town occasionally, this happy little family. I heard via the gossip mill years later that they added a boy to the brood. Yep, Caleb has it all now."

Phillip refrained from uttering the response that flew to the tip of his tongue: Caleb may appear to have it all, but not where his brains are concerned. Certainly not back then when the stupid ass let you go.

"What about you, Phillip?" she asked, interrupting his thought, "was Claudia your first love?"

"No, it wasn't anything like your story. I had a girlfriend in high school but I wouldn't call it love, not the kind I experienced later. Out of control teenage hormones, more likely, and it lasted well into that summer. Anyway, she left first, took off for a college in Minnesota and I went to Michigan State, just like my brother Gordon before me. Elaine and I stayed in close touch for a while, dated on breaks, but eventually we both found someone else. From the stories I've heard over the years about high school romances, ours was more typical."

"I think you're right. But then you met Claudia, and did she turn out to be your true love?"

"It didn't happen quite that way. I met Claudia much later, in my early thirties. Most guys of that era, including many of my friends, were married or at least engaged by then. Not me. It took me a long, long time to recover from a classic case of heartbreak. I fell really in love for the first time in my senior year at Michigan State with a girl who led me to believe she loved me too. You've heard that old saying, I trust, about how fools rush in where angels fear to tread? Well, you're looking at one of those fools. But it's all ancient history."

He took a last sip of coffee and she knew from the look on his face that he was not going to say any more about it. Subject closed. And it occurred to her that in some place deep inside him, he might never have fully recovered from that heartbreak, even after all those years.

As they approached her building, Karla asked if he would like to come up for an after-dinner drink. Her small bar, she said, was not all that lavish, but she could offer a decent port or come to think of it, she did have a seldom-requested bottle of Grand Marnier. She also kept on hand the makings for a Black Russian, the drink favored by her sister on her occasional visits.

"I'd love to. Believe it or not, the Black Russian just happens to be my favorite after-dinner drink. Like the Manhattan is my favorite cocktail. Maybe I'm a long-lost fourth cousin twice removed or some other obscure kind of relative." Whatever mood change had occurred at the restaurant was gone now.

She chuckled. "I like them too, but I don't make them for myself. Why don't you spoil me and make them tonight?"

They sat on the balcony and sipped their drinks in contented silence, savoring the cool late evening breeze and the view of the Key with its long necklace of glittering lights.

Phillip spoke first, tilting his head to indicate the display of stars and a perfect half-moon.

"I love the Florida sky. It's so clear, kind of like the pristine areas of northern Michigan. None of the pollution you get around cities."

"So do I, but what I really, really love are the clouds here. Especially in summer, when they get so huge and billowy. I see all sorts of things in their shapes. Sometimes a bearded old man, sometimes dogs. Most often a French poodle."

"I see mountains and nuclear explosions. How about that! I've found another cloud watcher."

"I've done that all my life, actually. But I never saw clouds in South Bend quite like the ones here."

"Neither did I in Michigan, and it's nice to find another Midwest transplant who appreciates a different kind of beauty. Once in a while, not very often, I run into someone who complains to high heaven that nothing here is as good as what they left up north."

"I haven't been here as long as you have, but I've run into people like that on the tennis courts. Sure it's hot, which is their usual gripe, and I sometimes gently remind them that this, not the place they left in

Chicago or New York, is where they can play tennis all year round. And I do wonder, with the really loud complainers, why they even moved here in the first place."

Phillip drained his glass and turned to her with a wink. "One word. Winter." He paused, then holding up his glass, asked if she would like another one.

"I don't think so, but please fix yourself another if you'd like."

"Thanks, but I think I'll be getting along. I really enjoyed the evening, Karla."

"And so did I, enormously." They were lingering at the door, not opening it. "Thanks for a lovely dinner, Phillip. I had the best time. The evening just flew by."

He smiled. "I was thinking the exact same thing. We must do it again, soon."

"Fine, but next time it's on me. If you want to take a chance on my non-gourmet cooking, that is."

"I'd love to." She had opened the door and was standing close to him. Somehow it seemed natural when he bent his head and kissed her. Her lips were warm and soft and Phillip drew away, reluctantly, backing into the hallway. Just before he stepped into the elevator, he turned to see her standing with her hand on the door, watching him.

Leaning toward the mirror over the bathroom sink for a closer look, toothbrush in hand, Phillip traced his lips with his left forefinger. He could still feel her mouth on his. He hadn't kissed a woman, not that kind of kiss since Claudia died. It felt exciting in its very unfamiliarity, sort of like wading into Lake Michigan when he was a boy after not being there since the previous summer's family camping trip. Forgetting how it was, then having it all come back with that first cold slap against his legs that prepared him for the headfirst plunge that felt so great he'd stay in the water until his mother waved him in for the picnic. He would head back to the beach, shaking the water out of his ears and hair, the sheer exhilaration of it making him laugh as he ran.

He'd rediscovered a very special and appealing sensation tonight when he kissed the lovely Karla. It made him realize how much he had missed the tender sweetness of a woman's lips. He hadn't forgotten how to kiss, oh no, and he smiled as he recalled the way she had clasped her hands around the back of his neck and pulled him closer after the first tentative touch. Face it, Phillip, he told the image in the mirror, that was no obligatory peck. That was a real kiss between a man and a woman, and it was pretty damned exciting.

He rinsed his face and remained standing, taking stock of his reflection. Not too bad for sixty-seven, he decided. His face was lined but not all that wrinkled, not like some of the people he'd seen around the pool who spent hours baking their faces and bodies in the hot sun in pursuit of an ever-deeper tan. Claudia had wisely decided before they moved to Florida that all the reading she had done about sun damage and skin cancer should alert them to the dangers of overdoing it, tempting as it was for winter-weary newcomers from the cold north. Most of all, she was avid about the necessity of using sun screen. She was faithful about it and got him to try it. He didn't like the slippery feeling it left but kept using it to please her. Now he didn't bother with it, mostly because he avoided the strongest rays by walking in the early mornings and swimming in the pool at sunset.

He ran his fingers through his hair. Mostly silver now, but here and there a thin streak of the old red, and a pretty full crop of it. He liked thinking of it as silver, a term his lady barber at the Hair Port used to describe it. It was a nice word, not as old-sounding as gray or white. It was receding a bit at the temples and forehead, but you couldn't say he was anywhere close to balding. Not as many curls anymore, more like waves, and easier to deal with than those wayward spirals that kept springing up no matter how much gel you used to try to calm them.

What is going on with you, Phillip, he asked the man looking back at him with the goofy smile. One little kiss and you're checking yourself out like a teenage girl. The thought made him chuckle and he turned away, but not before looking at his upper body, straight on and then sideways. He was grinning and shaking his head as he slipped into bed. In that hazy zone of half-wakefulness, he lay thinking that it had been a very long while since he'd gone to bed full of anticipation of seeing a woman again.

4

She called two days later to invite him to dinner. Phillip was headed for his walk when the phone rang and now, after talking to her, he felt a heightened burst of energy. The sun shone even brighter this fine October morning, and he called out greetings to other walkers and runners with an enthusiasm that generated broad smiles in return. From the beginning he was struck by the friendliness that abounded in Banyan Bay. Back in Pine Ridge people who knew each other tended to exchange friendly greetings, but of course that included almost everyone in town. Here, though, familiar face or not, it was the customary thing to do. He supposed it had a lot to do with the fact that many were retirees with lots of leisure time, and of course all that sunshine and balmy weather had to make you feel cheerful.

Claudia was the walking enthusiast, and at first he resisted her urgings to join him. After all those years of having to get up early to go to work, he allowed himself the luxury of sleeping in mornings. But after a while the novelty wore off and he began realizing that when Claudia returned from her walks she was full of energy. Eyes sparkling, she'd talk about meeting other walkers and runners, spotting various creatures in the wooded areas, and listening to the symphony of bird calls. Once he started joining her on those walks he caught her enthusiasm and began rising even earlier than she did to make coffee and as he put it, hit the road. After she died, walking alone had been very tough at first, but he was determined to force himself to keep at it.

The simple act of stepping out into sunshine and breathing fresh air helped enormously to lift his spirits. He started the lone walks slowly but soon began hitting his old energetic pace and best of all, responding to others along the way. And on days like today he was feeling especially grateful that he and Claudia had made the decision to move here.

Lost in musing, he rounded a familiar corner and came face to face with a couple he saw frequently on his walks. Nice people, always walking their two friendly dogs, a Schnauzer called Oscar and a Goldendoodle named Winnie. They paused in their conversation to greet him, and the dogs strained at their leashes, tails wagging. Phillip addressed each dog by name, then gave each a long affectionate rub. The Schnauzer, wanting more attention, barked at him as he walked away, and Phillip grinned. He loved dogs, grew up with them, but he and Claudia had never owned one. After she died, every now and then he thought about getting a dog to alleviate the loneliness in the condo, but that was the extent of it. Thus far he had not taken any action. No trip to the local shelter, no following up with phone calls when his interest was piqued by an occasional newspaper ad. His darling Claudia had been right. He really was Mister One of These Days.

He spotted a woman walking toward him far down on the other side of the street and almost instantaneously recognized the redhead. As always, she approached looking straight ahead, never breaking that brisk stride. Phillip did not turn to look at her after she passed him. Not today. He had always enjoyed looking at pretty girls, and Claudia never minded. At the beach, he liked observing those young things parading past wearing little more than strings and strips of cloths, all tanned and toned, waiting to be looked at by the young guys. In fact, if he was reading, she might nudge him and say "Babe alert. You're missing a good one," and he'd look up and smile. But today his mind was full of Karla Lynne Anderson and the delightful prospect of seeing her again, and soon.

5

As soon as she opened the door, the aroma sent Phillip's salivary glands into overdrive.

"Oh, my God! Is that what I think it is?"

"If you think that what it is, is good old American pot roast, then the answer is yes."

"Pot roast! My Mom used to make it all the time. I haven't had it in years. When I'd come home weekends from State, I'd smell it as soon as I came through the door, and make a beeline for the kitchen."

"Did Claudia make it too?"

"No, she was a great cook but pot roast was one of those things she didn't try, maybe because I talked so much about my Mom's. She may not have wanted to compete, I don't know. Anyway, this one smells a tad different than the one I remember, richer or something."

"Could be the wine. I use it pretty generously. I think it makes the gravy tastier and the meat especially tender. Speaking of which, what is in that fancy bag you're holding and are you going to stand there with it all night?"

"Sorry," he laughed. "I must have gotten carried away getting that whiff of your cooking. Anyway, the guy at the wine shop agreed that this is a very nice cabernet. It's one I'm familiar with. And I thought I'd also bring along a Sauvignon Blanc because I didn't know what you planned for dinner."

"Fine. We'll save it. We can have it when I do my special red snapper."

The food was delicious and Phillip loved everything about the dinner; the linen place mats that complemented the colors in the china, the crystal vase that held fresh flowers, the way the candles so perfectly framed and lit up Karla's lovely face across the table. After dinner they moved out to the balcony and sat quietly for a while, sipping hot fragrant coffee and enjoying the fresh breeze off the water. It was Karla who broke the silence.

"Phillip, I must tell you how happy I was when you showed up at my party. I hadn't gotten a call from you saying you weren't coming, so I more or less planned on seeing you, but I didn't know for sure. In case you wondered why you got an invitation from someone you didn't know, I sent it after I'd seen you walking a few times and noticed you were always alone. When you walked past Marnie's place that one morning when she'd invited me for coffee, I asked her if you were married. She told me all about you, how you had lost your wife a couple of years ago, and I decided I simply had to meet that incredibly handsome man. The wheels started turning in my head and I thought, I'll have a cocktail party and invite a bunch of people who have entertained me. And make sure I also invite Mr. Phillip Ashcroft!"

He took a minute to let that sink in before he responded.

"Well, listen to this. The day your invitation came I missed it at first because it was hidden in a bunch of junk mail, and it came this close to getting tossed into the recycle bin." He held up his hand with his thumb and index finger almost touching.

"No! Really, Phillip? You see, yours was the first invitation I sent and I waited to see if you would call with regrets. If you had, I would have postponed the party. When I didn't hear from you for a couple of days, I decided you were coming. It never would have occurred to me that you didn't get it. That was much too close!"

"I've been a lot more careful going through the mail ever since. But it all turned out great. I came to your party and here we are comparing notes about the whole thing, including my wondering, as I told you on our first date, if you had put me in a group labeled 'older men'. Not exactly in your father's age range but..."

"And you were so wrong. At any rate, I've always believed in the old wisdom that age is so much more than just a number. Haven't you known people who are old at thirty-five and others who are young at eighty? I have, and I bet you have too. It's not about numbers at all, it's how you feel about yourself and the way another person makes you feel. And speaking of that very thing, right now I'm feeling full of myself for having had the good sense to figure out a way to meet you."

Phillip rose, leaned over and kissed her. "And right this minute, I'm thinking that when I rescued your invitation, I actually considered calling you with regrets, and what a dumb-ass decision that would have been. I'd like to think we would have met sooner or later, but I'm so happy it was sooner, and at your party. We had time to spend together that evening, time enough for me to know I had to see you again."

They sat for a while, each lost in thought, saying little. Neither wanted the evening to end, yet neither moved to prolong it. It's too new, Phillip thought, too nice just the way it is to rush things. Better to take it easy, go slowly. He looked forward to the prospect of a real courtship, now that she'd told him she was attracted to him. But incredibly handsome? Now that was something. Not quite the way he perceived his looks, but he'd take it, and gratefully.

She walked to the door with him. He started to thank her for the dinner, but she stopped him, putting a finger to his lips. Then she wound her arms around his waist, lifted her head and kissed him, a much longer kiss this time, a kiss brimming with promise, a kiss that tempted him for a brief second to reconsider taking things slowly. Walking home in moonlight so bright he could see his shadow, he could still feel that kiss, so much more intense than the first. Look out, Phillip, you could get addicted to those lips very easily. He picked up his pace, surprising himself by whistling, something he hadn't done in years.

Later, he lay awake thinking how quickly things can change, how dramatic the transition from acceptance of the status quo, pleasant enough but undeniably lonely, to anticipation of an exciting new chapter in his life. No question, he was one very lucky guy. He certainly hit the jackpot the day Claudia said she'd marry him. No man could have asked for a better wife. It hadn't always been smooth sailing, of course, but all in all it was a very good marriage, much better than some he knew about among his friends and acquaintances.

And now look what had dropped in his lap. Ever since Claudia died, the likelihood of a relationship with another woman was so far from his mind, he gave it almost no thought. Then along came that little yellow envelope with its magical introduction to the lovely, bewitching Karla who tonight expressed how strongly she was attracted to him. He still felt somewhat incredulous, yet the way she looked at him made him believe her. Even though he hadn't known her all that long, he had a strong feeling she was someone he could trust. Phillip believed himself to be a good judge of character, a knack that had served him well in his business dealings, and trustworthiness was up there at the top of the list. It was an all-important attribute, not just in business but especially in matters of the heart, and Claudia had it in spades. He could trust her with anything, even telling her about Amanda. Not everything, of course. So much of it would remain forever between him and God.

Amanda. Now how had that name suddenly emerged, winging its way uninvited into his consciousness? Damn it, why had he allowed his mind to wander into territory he knew was dangerous, a minefield littered with painful memories he tried so hard to keep in a locked place in his heart. He should be drifting off into sweet slumber now, remembering the evening with Karla, anticipating the promise he had felt in her kiss. But it was too late. Sleep would not come anytime soon tonight. Phillip knew from long experience that even after all these years, there was no use fighting it. He was doomed once again to relive it, all of it. He lay on his back with his hands clasped behind his head, eyes open but not seeing the walls and ceiling lit by moonlight slanting through the partially open louvers. He was seeing his old house in East Lansing, just off the Michigan State campus.

6

They were seniors when she moved into the house next to the one he shared with his three best friends from high school. He remembered seeing her the year before around campus, mostly from a distance and almost always walking with different guys or a bunch of girlfriends. When he heard she was from Los Angeles, he wondered what a girl from sunny California was doing in a state well known for its long, brutal winters. And now she was his neighbor. The first time he saw her up close, she was lying stretched out on a blanket in her front yard, talking to Sabrina, one of the roommates he'd met when he moved in. That day both girls were wearing shorts and halter tops, taking advantage of the warm September sun for a last shot at a tan before the weather changed. The new girl had moved into the house very recently, replacing someone named Bunny who had just left, apparently because she didn't fit in with the other three. Phillip learned all this from Scott, the eagle-eyed roommate they called The Sheriff, who kept track of everyone and everything in their immediate area.

   He watched her for a while through the window above the kitchen sink, trying to decide whether or not he dared walk over and introduce himself. She really was a knockout, and that made him feel uncharacteristically shy about approaching her. But he did, finally, and Sabrina introduced them.

   "Amanda Stewart, meet our neighbor Phillip Ashcroft." She sat up, smiled and extended a sun-warmed hand.

"Hi, Phillip, nice to meet you. I've seen you around."

He felt like an idiot, holding her hand and staring. She was even more gorgeous up close. He couldn't seem to find his voice and it seemed to take forever before he spoke.

"Good to meet you, too." Slight pause. "Amanda." He let the name linger on his tongue, loving the sound of it.

She was very nice, ignoring Sabrina's barely-suppressed little giggle and inviting him to sit on the blanket. After a few minutes of conversation, Sabrina excused herself and went into the house. Sensing his nervousness, Amanda asked him casual questions about his background and interests, courses, his favorite sport. She was easy to talk to, and he gradually relaxed enough to carry on a conversation he hoped came across as reasonably normal. He was feeling far from normal, though, even after he was back in his house. He opened a book but found it impossible to concentrate on the printed page. Her face kept getting in the way. He had memorized so much of her while they sat talking. Her eyes were a shade of blue that made him think of the deep part of Lake Michigan. And that hair, a thick fall of chestnut brown that sparkled in the sun with little gold lights.

He would wonder later how he got up the nerve to ask her for a date, but he did. She said yes, and for that he offered thanks to whichever gods were in charge of such unlikely strokes of fortune. They saw a movie in town he had trouble concentrating on, and stopped for hamburgers and beer in a noisy bar afterwards. He couldn't stop looking at her face, couldn't tear his eyes away even though he realized she had to be thinking he was acting like the lovesick puppy he knew he was. He asked her out a couple of times after that first date, but she turned him down politely, saying she was busy. He convinced himself he'd blown it, had come across as small-town and unsophisticated, not like the guys he was sure she was used to in Los Angeles. He tried not thinking about her but it was impossible because he saw her every day, coming and going, and his nights were filled with dreams of her.

It was starting to get dark that evening in early October when he walked home from the library and saw her sitting on her porch step. She called his name as he approached his house, and walked over to where he stood clutching a stack of books. His heart had started pounding and he was feeling a little dizzy. She was wearing a dark blue sweater over sweat pants and it was still light enough for him to see it was the same color as her eyes. She smiled and said "I was waiting here hoping to catch you before you went inside. You didn't say I could have a rain check when I couldn't go out with you both of those times you asked me but…" she paused and he held his breath for what seemed forever until she added "I would like one now, if you have a spare." She kept smiling that killer smile, and it took a couple of seconds before he felt capable of keeping his voice reasonably casual when what he really wanted to do was jump up, throw the books in the air and shout for pure joy.

"Yep, I do happen to have one, now that you mention it. What about using it Friday night?"

October. The month filled with magic, the beginning of their love affair. They saw each other almost every night, watching TV, going for long walks along the Red Cedar River, having dinner at each other's house or at one of the cheap places in town. She was a decent cook when it came to things like macaroni and cheese or tuna casserole, and Phillip enjoyed grilling hamburgers and hot dogs in the nice weather that lingered all through that autumn. They were lovers by then, and Phillip couldn't stop marveling at his great good fortune. She wasn't just beautiful, she was warm and sweet and bright and fun to be with, and he couldn't understand what she could possibly see in him, this gangly guy with a mop of untamed curly red hair. A guy from a small town in Western Michigan whose parents had to work hard to send him and Gordon to college. She, who could have had her pick of those rich, sophisticated, smooth guys from Chicago or the wealthy suburbs around Detroit like Grosse Pointe and Bloomfield Hills.

On one of those rare Indian summer days a benevolent nature sometimes bestows on Michigan in late October, they sat on the river bank eating a picnic lunch and sharing stories of previous romantic attachments. Phillip went first. He'd gone steady with a girl named Elaine Ryker in high school, and the relationship continued through the summer after graduation. She was the first to leave, having decided upon the small college in Minnesota her mother had attended, and he followed Gordon's path at Michigan State. At first they kept in close contact, but gradually the intervals between phone calls and letters kept lengthening. By spring break they were dating other people and when she told him she was more than casually involved with someone else, he was neither surprised nor saddened. The news made him realize he no longer felt a truly romantic attachment to her. The breakup, such as it was, happened gently and without drama. There was an unspoken mutual acknowledgement that their high school romance was just that, and it had simply played itself out. In its wake a bond of friendship remained, and whenever they ran into each other back home, the encounters were pleasant and without any trace of regret.

Amanda's story was very different although she and Brett Caldwell were high school sweethearts too. His family had moved to Los Angeles from Houston at the beginning of his sophomore year, settling into a neighborhood in the same school district as Amanda's. It did not take long for the prettiest freshman to connect with the popular, good-looking transfer student from the school in Texas where he'd broken records as the football team's star quarterback. Unlike Phillip's and Elaine's romance, however, theirs only intensified after graduation. At UCLA they were inseparable. The Caldwell and Stewart families, especially the two mothers, formed a close friendship as their children's love affair progressed, and it seemed written in the stars that the young couple were destined to be married someday. But in the summer between his junior and senior years when Brett was an intern at a medium-sized advertising agency, all hell broke loose. Disaster struck in the shapely form of Denise Corning, former Hollywood starlet turned advertising executive. Eleven years older than Brett, she was still beautiful and glamorous. She set her sights on the young, handsome athlete and using her abundant sexuality as well as the irresistible lure of power, she had no problem drawing him into the web she so seductively spun. Caught, he offered no resistance. His problem was the increasingly difficult one of trying to balance time spent with two women, the girl he still loved and the woman who held him helpless in the thrall of lust. Later, Amanda would recall with disbelief her willingness to accept his excuses for breaking dates as working long hours nights and weekends to make himself an obvious choice for a permanent job after graduation. How, she would ask herself, could I have been such an unsuspecting innocent? No, scratch that, make it naïve and incredibly stupid. When inevitably he was caught in a network of lies, the game became impossible to continue and he was forced to confess the truth. Amanda was devastated, her perfect world with its perfect future shattered. She did not hesitate to spring into action on her immediate impulse, which was to put as much distance as possible between them. After doing some hasty research, she picked Michigan State University to apply for a transfer. East Lansing, Michigan appeared far enough away from Los Angeles, California to suit her purpose. And now, she told Phillip, just look at the way it had all worked out. She was in love with him, Phillip, and this time it was not the fantasy that was her much younger, immature conception of love. This was the real thing.

From October to May, each day took on a dreamlike status for Phillip. He found himself listening to love songs on the radio, lyrics surely composed for someone desperately in love. He read poetry in the library when he should have had his head buried in textbooks. It had been incredibly hard to concentrate on studying. Amanda was the more grounded one, and she set the rules for the time they could spend together. It was her disciplined, goal-oriented approach that kept him focused on graduating. But nothing could quench the yearning to be with her every hour of every day.

 They sat in her living room one windy March evening when her roommates were out, concocting a plan in great detail. Graduation loomed ever closer, and neither wanted to think about the impending separation. It helped to talk about what they would do to make being apart as brief as possible. First, the actual event. Amanda had learned in a recent phone call that her parents would not be able to come to the ceremony due to the rescheduling of an important combination business/pleasure trip to the Greek Islands. His parents, however, would be there just as they had attended Gordon's graduation. They had never met Amanda, but Phillip had told them so much about her that his mother had phoned to say they couldn't wait to meet her and have dinner afterwards with both of them.

 The next step of the plan involved asking his father to drive separately in his pickup and leave it at the house. That way, Phillip could help her the next day with packing and shipping, then drive her to the airport the following morning. When he had seen her off, he would load the truck with his belongings and come home for a couple of months. Enough time for Amanda to settle back into life at home and gradually impress the seriousness of their relationship upon her parents. A couple of months that would let Phillip find a temporary job which, combined with the money he'd saved from summer jobs going all the way back to high school, should cover the cost of a decent used car. Phillip was a familiar face at the bank, depositing paychecks, birthday and Christmas checks and withdrawing only small amounts from time to time for things he really wanted or for gifts for his family.

Then would come the best part, Phillip's actual arrival in the City of Angels. He loved the sobriquet, for was Amanda not his angel? And then there was this, another sign that the plan was as close to perfection as possible – he had, he was certain, a sure bet for a place to live. Dave Foyle, his best friend since high-school days, had dropped out of school after his sophomore year at State and moved to Los Angeles. He landed a good job with one of the aerospace giants, and the two young men stayed in touch, phoning each other frequently to discuss sports, weather and gossip about mutual acquaintances. Dave never failed to end their conversations with assurances that the door was always wide open for a visit from his old pal, and should Phillip decide to stay, he would be most welcome as a roommate in his spacious apartment in the Valley. Southern California, Dave assured him, was exploding with job opportunities these days, and Phillip could have his pick of whatever he wanted to do. So that part presented no problem, as far as he could tell. Once he secured the right job, he and Amanda could take all the time they needed to work out the details of the wedding. Already, he knew he would ask Dave to be his best man, and that gave the whole plan another layer of reality.

Satisfied with having worked out all the details, they toasted each other with cans of beer Phillip brought from the refrigerator. There was no doubt it would work out beautifully. For the immediate future, the best part was the precious time they would have together once his parents left. They would have the gift of that night, the next day and finally, the night before the temporary separation would begin. Now there was no need to be apprehensive about the coming of graduation. They would part for a brief period of perhaps two months, and even though it would seem like an eternity, afterwards they would be together for the rest of their lives.

7

The plan, so far, was going exceedingly well. The graduation ceremony proceeded smoothly and the speaker, a former respected senator from Michigan, delivered an unusually spirited, inspirational and not overlong address. Phillip's father, as requested, had driven the pickup and handed the keys to his son. His parents, especially his mother, seemed taken with Amanda's lovely manners and the appealing warmth of her personality. Both were drawn to her beauty, something he could tell by the way they kept stealing glances at her while trying not to be obvious about it.

The restaurant was filled with an air of gaiety as graduates and their families celebrated with good food and wine. The conversation at their table, full of congratulations and compliments, had flowed so easily that they were all surprised when his father looked at his watch and announced the hour. Hugs and tears were exchanged as Phillip and Amanda saw them off, and Phillip felt the genuine warmth that pervaded the atmosphere.

"I love them!" Amanda was still a bit teary-eyed as she watched the car disappear into traffic, her head resting against Phillip's shoulder. "I can tell they'll be great in-laws. I hope you'll feel the same about my parents."

The morning after graduation was devoted to packing Amanda's belongings and taking them into town for shipping. It didn't take long, since she had all of it organized with her characteristic efficiency. They brought her remaining travel items to his house, now empty of his roommates. There was plenty of time for him to buy a bottle of really good French champagne and put it in the refrigerator along with an assortment of cheeses. When he returned, Amanda insisted on going into town alone for a last chance to browse and shop. She bought a loaf of crusty French bread and a box of Belgian chocolates, smiling as she thought of Phillip's sweet tooth.

She had walked past the small wine shop a number of times, but never gone inside until now. She spotted a pair of champagne flutes with a sign marked "Clearance" beneath, and decided to buy them. Surely the occasion and the impressive bottle of champagne deserved those elegant glasses. When she picked them up with great care and brought them to the register, the clerk complimented her on her taste. She appeared to be a sixtyish woman with a plump, friendly face, her dyed black hair showing just a narrow strip of white at the part.

"These beauties are a real bargain, I just marked them down. Private party, huh? Not that it's any of my business."

"It's okay. Yes, very private."

"Must be the good-bye season. The town is just about emptied out. I sold a bottle of Moet to a young man just a little while ago and he said it was for him and his girlfriend. She must be something special. That's the most expensive one I carry."

"Curly red hair? Tall?"

The woman nodded. "Handsome too. And very nice. Lovely manners, you can tell when they come from good stock."

"That would be my boyfriend."

"Well, if you don't mind my saying so, now I see why he splurged on the Moet." She wrapped each flute in pink tissue paper and put them in a small box which she then carefully placed in a shopping bag.

Amanda paid her and reached for the bag, but the woman hesitated and set it back on the counter. She bent to retrieve a sparkly gold ribbon, took out the box and tied the ribbon around it, making a lovely bow with a flourish.

"Have a wonderful party, honey. You'll never be this young again." She smiled, looking wistful behind rhinestone-studded glasses shaped like cat's eyes. Then she handed her the bag and Amanda headed for the door, turning to wave as she walked out.

Her suitcase was packed except for the short silk nightgown she was wearing now and would toss in later. Her travel outfit hung in the closet next to Phillip's shirt and pants. It was a warm evening, and he wore only a pair of blue boxer shorts patterned with red hearts, her Valentine's Day gift to him. They sat close to each other on the sofa and didn't talk for a while, listening to the little radio he would take home with him tomorrow. Tomorrow, the very word they so carefully avoided saying. But this was now, and time to open the champagne.

   Phillip released the cork and they both laughed at the popping sound. He quickly covered the open top with his hand so none of the precious liquid could escape. He filled both flutes and they stood close to each other at the counter, toasting, sipping, and then kissing for a very long time. He studied her face, gathering her hair in both hands and sweeping it back. That glorious hair, longer than the current fashion, shiny chestnut brown shot through with gold in the light from the sun that was putting on a last-minute show before disappearing behind the trees. Her face, with its porcelain-fine skin and full lips that even in repose looked ready to smile. Those intensely blue eyes, so like the color of Lake Michigan far from shore where the depths seemed bottomless.

   "Phillip." She let out the breath she'd been holding. "You look as though you're memorizing my face."

   "I am. I need to."

   He picked up the flutes and set them on the coffee table in front of the sofa. She brought in cheese wedges and slices of bread artfully arranged on a plain white platter, and the bottle of Moet. They ate and drank and listened to the radio and kissed, long kisses that grew more urgent until he picked her up and carried her into the bedroom slowly and tenderly, lips locked.

   His bedside clock was the enemy that night and they tried in vain to ignore its soft relentless ticking. They clung to each other all night long as if terrified of letting go for even an instant. There was an undertone of desperation in their lovemaking, and it was more passionate than it had ever been, even at the beginning. Sleep arrived in brief interludes only when both succumbed to sheer exhaustion. Had a premonition of what lay ahead found its way into the very bones of these two? Was that what it was, a foreshadowing that this would be their last chance to make certain each curve and angle, each unique texture of the beloved's face and body would be embedded deeply into memory for all time to come?

At eight they left the twisted, rumpled sheets that Phillip would take home with him and launder, regretfully. He would much rather fold them and keep them with her scent intact in a secret place to treasure while they were apart. They showered together, washing each other with soapy hands. And then they made love for the last time, the warm water caressing their young bodies like spring rain.

Phillip stood at the glass wall in the terminal, watching her walk toward the plane. She was wearing a navy suit with a red and white striped blouse, and red high-heeled shoes. Her still-damp hair moved slightly in the breeze and she kept fluffing it with her free hand, the one that wasn't resting on the red purse that hung from her shoulder. She turned to wave midway to the plane and when she was on the top step, she waved again and blew a kiss just before the plane swallowed her. He tried to find her at one of the small windows, but failed. He stayed rooted to the spot watching the plane taxi down the runway, never taking his eyes off it until it lifted and disappeared into a cloud. Only then did he turn away and walk out of the terminal.

8

Phillip was sitting at his desk watching a parade of late afternoon dog walkers when he was struck by a spontaneous impulse to invite Karla for cocktails. They had been seeing each other for three weeks, having dinner at her place and in restaurants. So far she hadn't been here, and what better time than this evening, since Edna had arrived this morning to work her usual magic. Shortly after Claudia died, he'd hired the competent woman to give the place a monthly cleaning. He liked Edna. She was all business, no chatter, and he enjoyed the challenge of coaxing words out of her. Each time she came, she revealed a little more about herself and her roots, which Phillip found interesting and which gave him an insight into the good people in the nearby Amish community. They lived their lives modestly and honestly, always providing fair value for whatever goods or labor they provided.

Looking around at the meticulously clean rooms, he decided that yes, this would be a perfect time for Karla's first visit. He could fix a couple of drinks and something to munch on and then suggest running down to the shopping center for dinner at Salty Sam's. He picked up the phone and listened to the message on her answering machine, smiling at the sound of her voice. He told her he would like her to come for cocktails, asked her to return his call, then hung up.

When she hadn't called by six, he decided she was out for the evening, and made himself a Manhattan which he took into the den with a bowl of nuts. He switched on his favorite news show, and by the time he finished watching, it was full dark, a perfect backdrop for showcasing the brilliant display of stars he remembered watching back in Michigan with his mother all those years ago. How enchanted he'd been, listening to her calling out their names: Jupiter, Orion the Hunter, the Big Dipper, the Milky Way. It made him feel warm and special as he stood holding her hand in the darkness of their back yard.

Karla returned his call the next morning. She'd been visiting a woman in a retirement complex just south of Banyan Bay, she explained, and by the time she returned it was long past cocktail hour.

"When I heard your message, I thought darn, I wish I'd been there when you called. I went to visit Olive, who was a friend of my mother's, and it just happened that yesterday was her ninetieth birthday. I'm sorry, though, that I missed my chance to come to your place."

"That's nice to hear, but the lady must have loved seeing you on such a special day. How about tonight? Are you free by any chance?"

"You bet I am. What time? Can I bring appetizers?"

"Nope, but thanks. I want to try my hand at it. Oh yes, the time. How about five? Five-thirty?"

"Five-thirty sounds good. I have a tennis date this afternoon and that'll give me time to shower off the sweat and try to look presentable."

"I'm sure you look great even when you're sweaty. Do ladies sweat? I think I read somewhere that men sweat but ladies glisten."

"Really. Well, I run around that court pretty good and when I throw my outfit in the washer, I assure you there's plenty of glisten on it!"

Phillip laughed. "See you at five-thirty then."

He had probably overbought at Publix, but he was pleased with the way the assortment looked on the seldom-used oval china platter. Wedges of Jarlsberg, smoked Gouda and Canadian cheddar, pate with truffles, green and black olives, small gherkins and an assortment of crackers and little rounds of toast. Perfect. He was adding a shot glass filled with colorful toothpicks when it hit him, stopping him dead. That last night in East Lansing. He looked at the white leather sofa and the glass-topped coffee table but he was seeing the old tweed sofa with torn armrests, the rickety wood table that held the champagne bottle and the bread and wedges of cheese. Damn it, why did she have to keep resurfacing to torment him? Would he never be free of her, never stop wondering why she so cruelly shattered the dream she had convinced him was every bit as precious to her as it was to him?

The doorbell jolted him out of his unwelcome reverie, and he crossed the room swiftly to open the door. The sight of Karla standing there wiped everything else from his mind, and for a brief second they just stood smiling at each other. She looked so fresh, so appealing in white linen pants and a green and white tropical print shirt, holding a small white purse. She took a few steps inside, her eyes taking in the living room and screened lanai.

"What a lovely home, Phillip. You and Claudia did a superb job of decorating. It fits so perfectly with where we live. When I come into a home where the owners have tried to duplicate their place up north, it just doesn't come off somehow."

He smiled. "Thank you. When we bought this place, we looked around and found things that would complement the year-round greenery and flowers. Claudia didn't think the old, dark furniture, beautiful as it was, would look the same in this environment."

"She was right. But I notice you brought some treasures. Like that chair. I bet it has a story." She was pointing to an elaborately carved armchair with a red velvet seat.

"It does. My mother's grandfather was a cabinetmaker who knew a lot about wood and who admired fine workmanship. He saved enough money to buy it in Grand Rapids and presented it to his wife at Christmas one year."

As far back as he could remember, the chair had always been in the living room at home. When he and Gordon were children, his father took their picture sitting in it every year for the family Christmas card. Five years after his father died, his mother decided to sell the house and move in with Aunt Dorothy, her widowed sister. She asked her sons to choose whatever they wanted before turning the contents over to a friend who conducted estate sales. Among a handful of other pieces, Phillip and Claudia chose the chair, visualizing Christmas card photographs of the children they planned to have someday. Gordon was living in an apartment in Chicago then, and took very little, a few paintings, two crystal bowls and some silver pieces. He had always loved the Tiffany lamp, and their mother told him that although she planned to take it with her, she would be sure to leave it to Gordon.

Twilight was rapidly giving way to nightfall, and Phillip switched on the lamp nearest him. Karla sat next to him on the sofa, sipping her martini and complimenting him on the appetizers, which Phillip noticed she was eating with relish.

"I was just thinking about running down to Salty Sam's for dinner, if that sounds appealing to you," he said, "or maybe you'd prefer another place, maybe something not quite so casual? You look exceptionally lovely tonight."

"No, casual's good. But maybe we don't need to go out."

"You mean order in pizza?" He was grinning.

"Actually, I happen to love pizza, but I don't indulge all that often. I keep hearing it's good for you and I'm all for that except I do have to watch those annoying calories, darn it. Obviously you don't."

"Yeah, it's a hereditary thing, I guess. Slim genes."

"Lucky you. Tell you what, you've provided these delicious nibbles, so why not let me whip up something at my place? We can just walk over and I'm sure I can…"

"Absolutely not." He cut her off, his voice firm. "This is my treat. If it comes to that, I'm not all that bad in the kitchen, you know. I could rustle up something here."

"Okay, you're on. But only if I can help."

Moving around the small kitchen together had a comfortable feel to it, as though they had done this before. She seemed to know where to look for things, food and utensils alike. He was putting a salad together, tearing crisp leaves of romaine into small bits, adding thin slices of cucumber, grape tomatoes and feta cheese, then tossing the mixture with Greek dressing. Karla was across the room at the range, creating something that involved eggs, grated cheese, tomatoes, mushrooms and the remainder of a small ham. It smelled wonderful. He turned to watch her busily stirring, her back to him. She had a lovely figure, a trim waist with gently curving feminine hips. Her hair barely touched her shoulders and the overhead light picked up the shining blonde highlights. He resisted the urge to walk over and wrap his arms around her. Lately he had been thinking a lot about making love to her, but wanted to proceed cautiously. Early in their relationship she had talked about dating a few over-eager men after her divorce, and how their impatience to rush her into bed had turned her off. That sort of behavior mystified Phillip, always had. What pleasure was there in lovemaking that wasn't mutually desired? Both needed to be ready, and he felt certain he would know when that moment came with her. She most certainly had sent signals with those kisses that were growing more inviting each time their lips met.

He managed to find a couple of candles and two small pewter holders in a buffet drawer, and two white linen napkins. A pair of crystal wine glasses from the china cabinet held the chardonnay he had put in the refrigerator some weeks before and never opened. He lit the candles and sat back to enjoy the impromptu meal with a feeling of pure satisfaction. Laughing, they toasted each other and their fine team work, then ate the simple dinner as though they were dining in a fine restaurant.

"I don't know about you," Karla said, putting down her fork and dabbing at her mouth with the napkin, "but I thought that was delicious. I can't believe you had those nice fresh mushrooms on hand. You must be hiding a talent for cooking, and I don't mean ordinary bachelor fare. Great salad, too."

"Yes, I'd have to agree that it was delicious, but you were the one who put it together. I thought it was fun, scrounging around for the ingredients and each of us working our own station, just like cooking in a restaurant. Speaking of which, I am definitely not a chef, but once in a while I like to do little things like putting mushrooms in a skillet with some butter to go with a steak I might defrost and throw on the grill."

"See? You know how to saute. Your nightly meals can't all have been about frozen TV dinners, which you once told me you practically survived on!"

"Oh, that." He looked sheepish. "Well, maybe I exaggerated a bit to make you feel sorry for me so you'd invite me to more of those great dinners at your place."

They sat on the sofa drinking coffee and listening to some of his CDs. The room was filled with the magic that happens when artists like Sinatra and Fitzgerald give voice to the romantic, heartbreakingly beautiful songs of geniuses like Gershwin and Cole Porter. Phillip told her he was happy to learn that she appreciated his taste despite the difference in their ages.

"It has nothing to do with age, Phillip, and let's not go over that again. Some things are just timeless. Listen to the lyrics, they describe the way lovers have always felt, and always will feel. Songs like these will never go out of fashion."

"Ah," he said. "Casablanca. As Time Goes By."

"Exactly." She took his hand and very softly sang "Moonlight and love songs…never out of date…"

He firmly refused her offer to help clean up, and after finishing, he offered an after-dinner drink. She shook her head.

"No, thank you. I'm very content right now, and I don't need one more thing. I'm so glad we stayed in tonight, Phillip. Just the two of us. A perfect evening, but it isn't over yet."

Before he could respond she took his face in her hands and kissed him, a slow, deep, lingering kiss. He moved to embrace her, but she pushed him away very gently and reached for her purse on the end table. She withdrew a pink plastic tube, opened it and waved a toothbrush back and forth, smiling mischievously all the while.

9

One of the vertical louvers, the end one on the right, had always leaked a thin strip of light at dawn. At first neither said anything about it, but after a while Claudia had complained, saying that bedrooms should be completely dark early in the morning in case people wanted to sleep in.

"But we don't do that," Phillip pointed out. "I gave up sleeping in, remember? A long time ago, thanks to you. You turned me into a guy who loves to walk and we both know mornings are best for that, before the sun turns the temperature setting to broil."

"Doesn't matter," she answered with that pure feminine logic he found at once exasperating and endearing. "I'm talking about IF we wanted to sleep in."

Giving up, he tried adjusting it, but finally realized the problem was the damned thing was just a hair too narrow. He suggested leaving it alone and won his case when he convinced her it helped him wake up and make coffee. Bringing the hot fragrant cup to her in bed gave him the satisfaction of repaying her for all those years when she was the one who got up first, especially on those cold dark mornings in the long Michigan winters.

It was that narrow shaft of light which revealed the horror that greeted him one morning two years ago. As usual, he had slid quietly out of bed just as dawn was breaking, not wanting to awaken her. He loved the way she would sniff the coffee as he walked toward her, then smile, eyes closed, murmuring "Ah, my hero approaches to revive me."

But that terrible morning it was all wrong, so horribly wrong. In the faint strip of light he could see that her eyes were wide open, staring, and she wasn't making a sound.

"My God!" he had cried, almost dropping the coffee mug. "Claudia! Claudia! Sweetheart! Oh God, no!"

His hand trembled violently but he was able to hit the speed button to summon emergency help and then hurriedly find a weak pulse. She was alive when the EMS crew came, still alive when they put her in the ambulance. They told him she must have suffered a massive stroke sometime during the night. How, he wondered, could he have not been aware of it? As if reading his mind, the older one assured him they strike silently, without warning, and for the victim who didn't know it, mercifully. Had it occurred during the day, she would have had a chance of recovery with immediate treatment, but as it was, the outlook was grim. Phillip prayed as he held her hand in the ambulance, prayers he hadn't said in years but which sprang back as though he'd said them yesterday. He was holding her hand when the second stroke hit, the fatal one, just as the speeding vehicle approached the emergency entrance.

The hospital was on the main highway six miles north of Banyan Bay. How many times had he and Claudia driven past and remarked that so far luck had been with them, since neither had ever spent a single day in a hospital. They had gone into this one only once, to visit a neighbor who was recovering from cardiac surgery and both had been favorably impressed with the overall ambience. They agreed that when the inevitable day came when one of them needed to be hospitalized, this appeared to be a good one.

On that awful, surreal morning, Phillip sat in Brian McCullough's office, trying to grasp what the young doctor was saying. He spoke with a Midwestern accent and his brown eyes were compassionate as he attempted to tell Phillip in comprehensible terms exactly what had happened to Claudia. Phillip kept nodding, sure that he could absorb the words now and sort them out later. When it was clear the conversation was over, Phillip stood and shook the doctor's hand. Doctor McCullough told him that the hospital would refer him to a grief counselor if he wished, and that he would be welcomed into a therapy group for survivors that met monthly at the hospital. Phillip thanked him and said he would consider it. Then he walked out of the office, out of the hospital, and headed for home to make funeral arrangements. He and Claudia had discussed such matters long ago and agreed on cremation. He hadn't thought he would be the survivor, but here he was, alone in a world that Claudia had just left.

10

Now Phillip lay facing the window, and the wayward louver let in a sliver of bright light that told him it was midmorning, much later than when he usually woke up. He had to clear his head for an instant, long enough to realize he was not alone in the bed. Turning cautiously, he looked at Karla as she slept beside him, listening to her deep rhythmic breathing. A strand of blonde hair lay across her cheek, and he checked the impulse to move it, fearing he might disturb her. He lay very still and let his mind drift into a reverie, recalling every delectable moment of last night. Last night, when she'd smiled so provocatively and waved that toothbrush. He remembered feeling the years slip away with the clothes that she was impatiently removing from his body in the soft glow of the lamp he'd switched on as they entered the bedroom. His fingers trembled when it was his turn, and he undressed her slowly, taking time to fully appreciate each aspect of her womanly beauty. Their lovemaking was the culmination of desire that began almost the moment they met and grew stronger each time they were together, something both confessed in the lovely afterglow.

Smiling, still unable to let go of that sensation of wonderment, he slipped out of bed to start the coffeemaker. When he came back into the bedroom she was awake, stretching contentedly. Like a cat, Phillip thought, thinking of Flo, the cat he'd grown up with, the way she liked to stretch her sleek gray body as she lay in her favorite patch of sunlight.

"Good morning, lovely lady." He lifted the strand of hair from her cheek. She quickly ran her fingers through her hair and sat up.

"I probably look a mess!"

"No, you look absolutely beautiful." He sat on the bed and reached for her, kissing her. "Coffee here or in the living room?"

"Kitchen. Better still, how about your deck so we can watch the birds while we sip. Got a robe a girl could borrow?"

He started to get up, but she took hold of his arm, pulled him down toward her and said softly "But there's lots of time for coffee. Let's not rush."

****

It was almost noon when Phillip poured the last of the coffee into her mug as they sat watching a small group of roseate spoonbills foraging in the soft soil of the bank on the other side of the small lake. Karla gasped as one of the birds suddenly lifted its wings.

"Oh, look at that, Phillip! I've never seen a spoonbill until now, just pictures, and I didn't know the underside of their wings was that brilliant pink. What a gorgeous color!"

"Yes, it is a pretty spectacular sight. These birds don't show up all that often, I think this might be only the third time I've seen them here. They came today just for you, my lady." She smiled and put her hand on his arm. He picked it up and kissed it, then said "I don't know about you, but I'm starving. Let me see what I can whip up for breakfast, or is it time for lunch?"

"Both," she laughed, "which is why it's called brunch. But no, I insist on making it at my place. You've been quite the gracious host, cocktails, dinner, and…everything. I especially loved the 'everything'."

"Yes," he said solemnly, his voice hoarsened, "the 'everything'."

They were crossing Banyan Bay Boulevard holding hands, when the redhead appeared just ahead, walking north. Phillip paused midway and when Karla looked at him questioningly, he asked if she knew the woman. She shook her head.

"No, but I see her walking a lot, and she goes at a pretty fast clip. Seems to be kind of a loner. Nobody I talk to seems to know much about her, but she has been seen swimming in the early evening when she has the pool pretty much to herself. She must be a real fitness buff.

Why do you ask?"

"I don't know. She walks past my place a lot and seems to be looking for an address or something. It's none of my business, I just keep noticing her."

"It's that red hair I bet, and she's pretty, as I'm sure you've noticed. Great body too. But she's too young for you, Phillip. Or should I be jealous?"

"Sure, go right ahead. How flattering!" He laughed, adding "I really can't tell how pretty she is or isn't, the way she hides behind those gigantic sunglasses. But I am a mere man so of course I have noticed the body. Almost," he fixed her with a comical leer, "as great as yours, and I can state that now with certainty based on first-hand knowledge."

She gave his bare leg a playful kick with the side of her foot.

"You're not going to brag to the guys at the bowling alley, are you? But okay, I'll accept the compliment. And don't you dare add that old caveat 'for a woman your age'!"

He squeezed her hand and they hurried the rest of the way, laughing.

11

Phillip spent Thanksgiving Day serving dinner at the Salvation Army. He had done it twice after Claudia died, politely declining invitations from neighbors who asked him to join them and any family members who happened to be visiting. This year Karla invited him to join her on her traditional holiday visit with June and her children in South Bend. She had bought her plane ticket in September, she explained, and now the thought occurred to her that he might enjoy coming with her.

"My sister would love to meet you, I know. She sounded very happy when I told her about us. I know you'd like her."

"I'm sure I would, and I appreciate your asking, Karla, but this is something I look forward to every year."

And he did, even though the sadness he felt looking into the faces of the people whose plates he filled remained with him for a long while afterward. Most were lone men, but last year there were quite a few women and a dozen or more children, some very young.

This year he was unprepared for the size of the crowd, at least twice as large as last year's, and it included even more children. He watched their eyes as he ladled gravy onto mounds of mashed potatoes and slices of turkey. The way those eyes fastened on the growing bounty on their plates, wide with anticipation of digging in! Fortunately, enough tables and chairs were available, some borrowed from a nearby church.

A thin man with a salt and pepper beard looked directly at him, and

Phillip recognized the veteran he saw regularly on his shopping trips to Publix, always sitting a few yards from the doors. One day he had introduced himself to Phillip, and Phillip suddenly remembered his name. He smiled at the man as he began filling his plate.

"Art! Remember we met a while back? I'm Phillip Ashcroft. How are you doing?"

Pleased to hear that Phillip knew his name, Art grinned, a wide grin showing several gaps between stained teeth.

"Doin' okay, man. How's it goin' with you?"

"Good, Art, good. Enjoy your meal." Phillip watched him move down the line, then began filling a plate for an elderly woman.

When everyone had been served, some of the volunteers stayed to eat but most left to be with their families. Phillip stayed, casing the room until he found Art sitting at a table with a man, woman, two boys and a very young girl. He pulled up a chair and sat next to Art, who was eating slowly, as though trying to make the meal last longer. Phillip considered starting a conversation, but the adults avoided looking at him. Shyness, perhaps, recognizing Phillip as one of the volunteers. Or more likely, embarrassment. He wished he could let them know the depth of the honor felt by the entire staff and for that matter, the whole of the Salvation Army, to be able to offer help in times of need. He did detect an eagerness to talk in the little girl who looked as though she was around five years old, and she gave him a bright smile.

"Happy Thanksgiving," Phillip ventured, and she started to repeat the words, but a stern look from her father quieted her. Phillip decided to let them eat in peace. Art, however, was a different story. He wanted to talk, and Phillip was a willing listener. He learned that Art had come to Florida ten years ago to escape the brutal winters and a bad ending to a relationship in the Upper Peninsula, where he'd lived most of his life. His special lady, he told Phillip, had run off with a guy, a drifter, who worked at a local bar. Not that he blamed her, he said, he was no prize package himself. He was candid about his addictions and said he was thinking about trying another rehab program. The last one had worked for a while and he even got a job at a fast food place for a while. When Phillip finished his meal, he shook Art's hand, slipping a twenty into it. He hoped he wouldn't use it to buy alcohol, but knew he probably would. Art stared at the bill for a moment before speaking.

"Aw, man, Mr. Phillip…I forgot your last name…"

"Ashcroft, Art, but please call me Phillip. And I hope you do more than just think about another rehab program."

"Okay then…Phillip. You're a true gentleman for sure. I don't know how to thank you. I want you to know, I promise you, I sure by God will talk to this guy who helps me out at social services about givin' rehab another shot. It worked that one time, anyway."

"That would be all the thanks I need, Art. Sometimes you just have to keep at it. You're a good man, and I hope people never stop thanking you for serving your country. You certainly have my thanks."

The father of the small family spoke for the first time, looking at Art and saying "Amen to that, friend."

Then Phillip said goodbye to the group and left with Art thanking him over and over, wet eyes following him all the way out the door.

12

Phillip found himself counting the hours of the last two days Karla was in Indiana, and he was so eager for her return he arrived at the airport in Tampa well ahead of the scheduled landing. Each time the tram pulled in with deplaning passengers he laid aside the magazine he wasn't really reading anyway to search for her. And there she was, finally. He spotted her immediately in the crowd when she got off, her blonde hair a beacon in the brightly-lit terminal. He reached for her carry-on bag and drew her into his arms in a single swift motion. God, he was glad to see her, hold her, inhale her scent and kiss those lips.

Halfway home, he suggested stopping for dinner at a restaurant just ahead that was famous for its impressive array of crab dishes.

"Sounds wonderful, but not as wonderful as home. Let's just get there as fast as the law allows. I love my sister, I adore my niece and nephew, and we had a lot of fun, but five days seemed too many because I missed you so much! I think we all were ready for the visit to end, as nice as it was. I may have talked June's ear off about you."

"And I missed you! Hell, I've been sitting in that airport for at least an hour because I couldn't wait to see you. Promise you won't go away again anytime soon."

"I promise. Now about dinner. The pretzels were fine, I think I ate at least three bags full of them, but I need actual food, badly! I know, let's pick up a couple of those great Cuban sandwiches from Tia

Lena's. We'll open that bottle of Chilean wine you brought over a couple of weeks ago, and just kick back and relax. That's my vision of pure heaven right now."

After dinner they sat on the balcony with their deck chairs touching, a soft woolen throw covering them both against the chill. A thin layer of fog diffused the lights from the boats on the bay and the buildings on the Key, and they sat watching for a while in contented silence. Then Phillip reached for her hand in the semi-darkness and cleared his throat. When he spoke, there was a tremor in his voice, and he was looking out into the night.

"Karla, I did a lot of thinking while you were away. About you. About us. I haven't said this before now, but something tells me you must know it. Heaven help me, I've gone and fallen head over heels in love with you."

She didn't say anything and still staring straight ahead, he said "Oh my God, I can't believe I just said that. I never thought I'd hear myself say those words again, not in this lifetime."

She reached for his face with both hands and turned it toward hers.

"Phillip. Listen to me. I've been waiting and waiting for you to say those words, you have no idea how long. I've been in love with you from the very first, my darling, but I was afraid to tell you, afraid I'd scare you off, even though I was pretty sure you felt the same…"

She paused for breath and he silenced her with a deep, lingering kiss. No more words were spoken. Rising together, they moved slowly into the living room and turned off the lights. Outside, the moon was shining softly through the haze, creating a dreamlike glow in the bedroom as they undressed and then lay between lavender-scented sheets, lost in each other in the long misty December night.

13

Karla had made French toast and crisp bacon for breakfast, and now they sat on the balcony drinking coffee and nibbling at a coffee cake she had taken from the freezer and warmed in the oven.

"Phillip, do you realize we're about to spend our first Christmas together? What about Gordon? Do you plan to invite him to visit you for Christmas? Does he usually come then? I mean Chicago is so cold right now, I would think he'd love to enjoy the beach and some nice warm sunshine."

"No, I don't think so. Claudia and I asked him the first year we were here, but he and his partner like to spend the holidays in their favorite spot in St. Thomas."

"His partner? Phillip, is he gay? You haven't told me much about your brother and I just assumed there was some kind of rift, so I didn't press you about it."

"No, nothing you could call a rift." Phillip cut a small slice of cake and ate it before he continued. "And yes, my brother is gay. Now the word 'gay' I find interesting." He waited while Karla refilled his cup before continuing.

"It's a word that had an entirely different meaning when I was growing up. It meant happy or joyful. It never would have applied to Gordon. There was an air of sadness about him. My parents called him moody but I saw something deeper early on. When we were both in our twenties and he had moved to Chicago, he told me a little about his struggles pretending to be like the rest of the family and his friends. He never really dated but he did some of the obligatory things like asking a girl to the senior prom. It had to be so tough for him. I'm glad things have changed so that today people are allowed to be who they are, openly."

"I did wonder why you didn't talk about him the way I talk about June. I just figured you two weren't close like we are."

"We are, but not in the same sense as you and your sister. I mean we never lose contact with each other for long but we seldom see each other. We're brothers, though, and that bond is there forever. But his lifestyle is very different from mine. With his interests and all the traveling he and Randolph do, we are actually together only on the rarest of occasions, the last one being Claudia's memorial service. He is also extremely involved with Randolph's family. Unlike my parents, who tried unsuccessfully to hide their disappointment when they found out my brother was gay, his partner's family were very accepting of their son's proclivity from the start. And when they met my brother, they fell in love with him. I was at their place once when Randolph's parents and sister stopped in for a visit, and I liked them very much. It's an old Chicago family with major old Chicago money as well, and they are very generous when it comes to providing their children with luxuries they might not be able to afford on their own. I should tell you that doesn't happen often with Randolph because he is a fairly well-known painter and owns a small gallery on the Near North Side, not far from their beautiful sky-high condo. Claudia and I visited them once, and you should see their amazing view of Lake Michigan. They both do very well as far as money is concerned. Randolph has a wealthy clientele willing to pay handsomely for his paintings and my brother shoulders his share of the expenses with the income from his line of work, which is designing furniture meant for fabulous North Shore mansions."

"You do sound okay with his lifestyle, Phillip. Did your parents ever come around to some kind of acceptance?"

"Oh yes. By the time of their passing – my mother died first at eighty, my father followed two years later -- things had gotten much better between them and Gordon. After a while the shock of learning their firstborn son was gay started to diminish. My mother was the first to understand the tragic price of severing the unique and beautiful connection between parent and child, and decide to discuss it with her pastor. That good man wisely sent her to another church where a group of parents in the same situation met for monthly discussions. She got my father to come too, and it really turned out to be a great help. I do know how deeply they regretted not having grandchildren fathered by Gordon. I thought Claudia and I could fulfill that wish, but as I've told you, that did not happen."

"I guess most parents think about that as they get older and their children grow up, the perpetuating of the family, whether by biology or adoption. I know how thrilled my parents were when my sister's Jake and then Felicia came along, and I knew how they grieved with us when I suffered each miscarriage. But back to Gordon. You've accepted his lifestyle, and you sound happy for him. You are, aren't you?"

"I am, Karla. Would I prefer to have a sister-in-law and her relatives, a nice big extended family? Nieces and nephews I could spoil, who would love their doting Uncle Phillip? You bet I would. But it wasn't in the cards, and as my mother always used to say, it is what it is."

"Honest answer, thank you. I know firsthand how important that is, having a very special relationship with someone who calls you aunt or uncle. I am Auntie Karla, they still call me that and I cherish it. I intervened when June hesitated about Felicia having her ears pierced when she was nine, something she really wanted, and when I finally convinced my sister to let her do it...well, I became her hero forever. Jake, well, that cuddly baby is a big handsome hunk now but never stopped introducing me to his buddies as his cool Auntie Karla. I was there with my parents when each kid first saw the light of day. And although Caleb was not on the scene either time, still he was very excited each time he became an uncle."

"Yeah, I have to admit I would have loved being an uncle. And I know Gordon probably would have loved it if Claudia and I had been able to have kids. As it is, he has a great life. A loving partner, work he enjoys, and an extremely busy social life. He and Randolph have a huge circle of friends – gay, straight, men, women, different ethnic backgrounds, different races, varied professions. They also share a love of travel, on the go so much that I sometimes wonder if they'll run out of new places to visit anytime soon."

"Well, when that happens, then they'll revisit their favorites, won't they? Gordon sounds like a happy man, and that's what's important."

"As I said, he couldn't be happier and God knows he deserves to be, after all he had to contend with in his youth."

"I'm glad to learn so much about Gordon, and I look forward to meeting him someday. Does he know about me? Us, I should say."

"He does, and he's very happy for me. I tried to describe you to him but he insists on a picture, so I'll have to oblige. And you will meet him, I promise. We'll plan a trip to Chicago so we can visit both of them."

"Fair enough. You've shown me his picture in your album, and I must say he is certainly a handsome man. Not more so than you, though."

"Thanks, but most of my younger years, I knew he was the standout. People, girls especially, always talked about my handsome older brother."

"Were you annoyed? Jealous? Maybe just a wee bit?"

"Yeah, but I think I managed to hide it. Gordon was my hero. I really looked up to him. And I still do, to this day. As I said, he and I live different lives and I may not understand it completely but I feel good knowing he is happy. He is loved by the person he loves, and what could be better than that? For any of us. God knows how grateful I am to have you in my life for that very reason."

Close to tears, she rose and stood behind him, bending to press her cheek against his, her arms circling his neck, and whispered "You are so full of compassion and you understand what love is really all about better than anyone I've ever known. Is it any wonder that I fell in love with you almost from the first, and the more I get to know you, the more I love you?"

14

Phillip sat at his desk, looking out the window at a sky that was rapidly darkening, and shuffling papers without really looking at them. He should be going through them in preparation for the next monthly board meeting just days away, but he kept losing his concentration. His thoughts kept wandering to Karla. Fact was, they hadn't seen each other for a couple of days and he missed her. He was smitten all right, and the self-admission made him grin. He stashed the papers in a file folder and slammed the drawer shut. To hell with all these documents and minutes and things, he'd call her and suggest running down to Salty Sam's for a drink and dinner. She didn't answer, so he left a message asking her to return his call.

A half hour went by, then another. It was almost eight and she still hadn't called. He realized he was hungry. Lunch had been earlier than usual today because he'd had to meet with someone from the state about an owner violating an environmental regulation. Seems the idiot had hired a service to trim some protected mangroves to facilitate his view without getting permission. Now he'd have to try to straighten out the damned dilemma. He'd give her another half hour and if she hadn't called by then, he'd just go by himself and have one of those tasty grouper sandwiches with fries and coleslaw, and a beer. She probably got hung up somewhere. Maybe her mother's friend at the retirement place needed her for some reason, and she wasn't back yet.

Salty Sam's was quiet and low-key for a change, the volume lower than usual on the multiple TV sets. Happy hour was over and the dinner crowd had begun to thin out. The regulars who showed up like clockwork to settle in for an evening of uninterrupted drinking and conversation hadn't started dribbling in yet. Phillip gave his order to the new young waiter and scanned the room, noting just a handful of couples scattered among the small tables.

Great sandwich, and the beer was perfect with it. It occurred to him not for the first time how nice it was to have a friendly place like this so close, practically right in the neighborhood. Chewing contentedly, he looked around the room again now that his eyes had adjusted to the dimness. And found himself on the verge of choking when he took a second look at one of the women and it struck him that it was Karla. She was sitting with her back to him. At first he thought he'd mistaken someone else for her, but then she turned her head slightly so that he caught enough of her face, those cheekbones, to know it couldn't be anyone else. His vision was still excellent, and he saw her companion very clearly. A man in his fifties, probably, with thick, longish black hair streaked generously with gray. Good-looking guy, from what Phillip could make out. He seemed to be doing most of the talking, looking at Karla very intently while she mostly nodded with occasional shrugs. Who was he, Phillip wondered, possibly someone from her past who had gotten hold of her address and dropped in to see her? As he watched, the man reached for her hand and kept it in his. They weren't eating, at least not now, and the man lifted a glass to his mouth with his free hand. He assumed she had a drink in front of her, too, but couldn't tell for sure. But oh look, now she gripped his arm with her other hand.

He tried not to stare but it didn't matter because Karla's companion was so focused on her he couldn't have been aware of anyone else in the room. Feeling suddenly lightheaded, Phillip pushed his half-eaten sandwich aside, almost knocking over the glass that was still half full of beer. The waiter rushed over at his signal and he placed a bill on top of the check as he got up, leaving the young man wide-eyed at the size of the tip. Then he headed for the door, almost tripping on the step as he hurried out.

He drove into his garage, got out and stood for a few minutes on the driveway. He started walking toward the front door, then turned abruptly and headed for Bayview Way. Clouds obscured the quarter moon and Phillip was glad of the darkness. He was going to spy on her and felt ashamed, yet powerless to stop himself. When he reached the gazebo next to the small lake in front of her building, he climbed the four steps and sat on the bench, breathing heavily. He wiped the sweat off his forehead with his shirt sleeve and positioned himself so that he had a view of the guest parking area a few yards to his right.

    He was hidden in the shadow cast by the roof, and he kept looking at the luminous face of his watch as cars pulled in and out of the parking spaces. Busy tonight. The first wave of snowbirds after Thanksgiving, most likely. Now forty minutes had gone by since he sat down. Where the hell was she, or more specifically, where the hell were they? Had they gone off to a place where he was staying, assuming he was someone from out of town? He was struggling to push away the image of her alone with the guy with all the hair in a hotel room, when finally a car pulled into a guest parking space and the man got out. Phillip could see him plainly before the headlights went off as he walked quickly around the front of the car to open Karla's door. He watched them walk through the glass doors into the lobby and disappear into the elevator, no good night at the front door like he was foolishly hoping would happen. He sat there for an hour, checking his watch, his mind spinning. Where was he, that guy, why wasn't he coming out of the building if he had seen her all the way up to her door, even if he came in for a drink the way he had after their first date? He was feeling chilled and looking at his watch again, saw that another hour had passed. It was getting on toward midnight, and what the hell was he doing huddled there shivering in the cold dark anyway? Disgusted with his own idiocy, he left then and half-ran the short distance home as though he was being chased, his heart pounding.

    Fool, he said aloud to his face in the mirror, remembering how he'd smiled at his image after that first real kiss. Goddamned old fool. How could he have imagined she would not have men chasing after her, a beautiful woman like her? He'd probably happened along during a dry spell in her dating life. After all, she hadn't been here very long and maybe now that she was settled, former lovers were starting to come out of the woodwork. Or maybe her story about that visit to an elderly woman was just that, a story, and she'd really been with this guy. Could be he was someone who came to town on business from time to time. Meanwhile, she probably thought he, Phillip, was acceptable as someone to go out with, even sleep with, until something better came along. And a woman could convince you she loved you all the while she was lying, as he knew only too well from having been so badly burned by Amanda all those years ago. Maybe it went hand in hand, being beautiful and being one hell of an actress.

   He was feeling bone-weary all of a sudden, and old. Very, very old. He was ready for bed but knew sleep wouldn't come easily tonight, so he poured bourbon into a water glass, never mind fussing with making a Manhattan right now. He needed a quick fix. He settled on the sofa in front of the television set, flipping the remote to the old movie channel. He didn't really watch the film, knew he would not be able to concentrate, nor did he care. But at least the black and white images provided a visual distraction, and kept him from running out into the street to howl at the moon.

He woke with the mother of all headaches just before dawn and gulped down a couple of aspirins. Get back into bed and sleep it off, he told himself, but something made him pull on his clothes and direct his feet right to the spot he was powerless to avoid. It was barely light enough to see the lake but beyond it, the parking lot light that was still on revealed the gazebo and all too clearly, the car parked four spaces from it. Sonofabitch. Still there this early morning, its owner undoubtedly sleeping blissfully beside her between those lavender-smelling sheets.

Karla returned his call late in the afternoon. He let the answering machine pick it up, jolted by the sound of her voice. He had a massive headache and for the first time in months stayed inside all day, foregoing the walk he almost never missed. She left a message asking him to call her back. Damned if he would. Not after what he'd seen last night. No matter what kind of excuse she might have, was he going to believe her or his lying eyes? He knew she didn't have a brother so she couldn't pull that one on him and besides, no cousin or other relative looked at a woman the way this guy was looking at her. No, he was done. Just like Amanda. Women. They were all alike, except for Claudia.

   His head was still throbbing painfully so he swallowed two more aspirins, glancing at himself in the mirror over the sink. He looked like hell. Well, Phillip, you've been had again, and you have only your stupid self to blame. Oh yes, this one was so convincing. Like that night when you told her about Gordon and she said she just keeps on falling more in love with you. Forget that bullshit, that's all it was. Just think about all the time you had with Claudia, one-in-a-million Claudia, and live out the rest of your years being grateful you had her as long as you did. You don't need to relive the agony Amanda put you through. Once was enough.

Karla called again around eight as he sat in front of the television set, eating a tasteless frozen dinner he'd zapped in the microwave. He listened to her message.

"Phillip? Are you okay? I called you this afternoon and left a message. I thought you might be out walking." Pause. "Okay, I'm home, so call me when you get this. 'Bye."

Oh, such a sweet voice. Yes, sure I'll call you. When hell freezes over, and maybe not even then. No bourbon tonight. But before he went to bed, he swallowed one of the prescription sleeping pills the doctor had ordered for him right after Claudia died. Long past the expiration date but who cares? Might make the medicine more potent, which would be fine with him. It took a long while before it worked, long enough to flood his brain with the memory of the betrayal Amanda had handed him all those many years ago. A memory he was helpless to resist, because what he had witnessed last night and early this morning brought it all back.

15

How confident he'd been, walking out of the terminal that last morning, so full of certainty that Amanda would be back in his arms within two months. He began the drive home in a state of elation, still riding the high of the incredible lovemaking, too exhilarated to feel any weariness from lack of sleep. It wasn't until he walked in the door that he realized he was starting to feel tired and very, very hungry. After greeting his parents, he was more than ready for the bacon and eggs and hash brown potatoes his mother insisted on cooking for him.

  The food and a couple of mugs of coffee revived him, and he told them about his proposed trip to Los Angeles. He was careful to leave out the part about moving there, deciding that could wait till later. For now, he told them he was looking forward to a vacation and would finally accept Dave's invitation to visit. His mother thought it was a fine idea and said so as she placed a platter of doughnuts on the table and sat next to him.

  "And you'll have that lovely girl to spend time with, Phillip. Your dad and I were so impressed with Amanda. She's beautiful, and she has a warmth you feel as soon as you meet her. Talking with her, I could tell she is also a very bright young woman. Who knows, dear, you just might end up moving out there and marrying her. Although we'd certainly miss you if that should happen. Heavens, you'd be almost half a continent away from us."

  Before Phillip could respond, his father said "Let's not rush things,

Sarah. Phillip has just graduated, and here you are planning his future, wife and all." He turned to his son. "Take your time, Phillip. You don't have to look too far ahead, your life is just beginning. If you did decide to move and settle down in another part of the country, well, we'd accept that as we did Gordon's decision to move to Chicago. Not that we see much of him, as close as it is…"

His eyes clouded over and Phillip quickly brought the subject back to the present.

"I'm not planning to fly out there right away, Dad." Careful, he reminded himself, this is part of the plan and it has to stay between you and Amanda for now. He waited a beat before going on.

"I thought I'd work for a couple of months, probably my old job at Tom's Tavern. Tom was always happy to take me on summers when I was home from school. That way I could add a little more to what I already have in the bank, and it's possible I could afford a decent used car and drive out there."

"Sounds like a good idea, actually. I've always wanted to make that drive across our beautiful country. Your mother and I were planning to do just that a long time ago. We said as soon as we could scrape up the money we'd go before we started a family. But then, wouldn't you know it, Gordon decided to let us know he was on the way. Your poor mother really suffered with morning sickness the first couple of months and that was that, as far as a long car trip was concerned."

"I never knew that, Dad, I mean that you wanted to make that drive."

"Well, I'm not too old to still do it." He refilled his mug and reached for a doughnut. "But in the meantime, we plan to give you a check as a graduation gift, to use any way you want to. Times have been good for us, and I think that our gift plus what you've saved up will get you a pretty good car with enough left over for expenses and some fun to boot. I have to compliment you, Phillip, on the way you've always handled money. You never wasted it the way a lot of kids your age did. I used to get a kick out of watching you sock it away. You reminded me of Patches, remember how hard she worked at storing nuts in the fall?" Phillip nodded, smiling at the memory of their pet squirrel, and his father waited a bit before asking "But are you sure you don't want to do this sooner? Do you really want to postpone it a couple of months?"

"Listen, Dad. You too, Mom. First of all, you don't have to do this. I don't have to tell you how much I appreciate your generosity. Not just for the gift you're about to give me, but for everything you did for both of us, all the sacrifices you made to give us a great life and a good solid college education. You just said some things that mean a lot to me, Dad, about the way I saved money, but the truth is, you and Mom gave me so much that there wasn't any real reason for me to go out and spend my own money. You gave me all I needed or wanted, and I know Gordon feels the same way. I don't want to jump right into job-hunting, but on the other hand I don't want to just lounge around. I thought I'd take a breather after getting out of school, spend time with both of you and some of my old buddies, work for a while. Then who knows where I may end up? Maybe here, maybe California if I find I like it there." He hoped he sounded casual.

His mother smiled as she refilled his coffee mug.

"I like your idea, Phillip. I have to admit it gives me a nice feeling, knowing I can look forward to having you all to ourselves for a while. We missed you, you know."

He lasted exactly four and a half weeks that seemed much longer. He missed her. God, how he missed her, how he ached for the sight of her, the touch of her, the smell of her hair. But something much more urgent had begun to get to him lately. It was the little furry caterpillar of unease that had started to crawl ever so slowly across his heart. The lovers talked every day, and at first the wires fairly pulsated with their passionate exchanges. But talking to her the last couple of weeks, he had picked up a very subtle, barely discernible difference in her voice and sometimes in her words. A hesitancy, a moderating of the ardor that had flooded his eager ears right after she returned home. Worse, he had to come to grips with the fact that it was becoming more obvious each time they talked.

He made up his mind on a Saturday morning in early summer. He couldn't put it off any longer, he had to call her, let her know he was coming out as soon as he could get a seat on a flight. Forget the car trip, he could come back and arrange that later, but right now he was driven by the intense need to see her, talk to her in person and find out what was going on. A knot was starting to grow in his gut and it was getting harder to act as though nothing was wrong, although he did catch an occasional glimmer of concern in his mother's eyes. He picked up the phone, his heart hammering in his ears.

"Hi, darling," he began, forcing a note of cheer he didn't feel, "I miss you so much, I just had to hear your voice so I can get through the day. Sorry it's so early, hope I didn't wake you up." She didn't respond immediately, and when she did her voice sounded subdued.

"Oh." Slight, almost imperceptible pause, but he caught it. "Good morning, Phillip. You didn't wake me. It's early, but I've been up a couple of hours. I'm always glad to hear your voice too." Lame, he thought, no greetings of endearment, no excitement. He was right, something very definitely was changing, and that gave him the impetus he needed to plunge right in.

"Listen, Amanda, I know we agreed to give it a couple of months, but here's the thing. I can't wait it out any longer. I thought I could when we planned the whole thing back in March, but I didn't know how it would actually feel, being away from you. Right now it seems like forever since I saw you off that last morning."

She started to say something but he cut her off, his words tumbling over each other.

"No, let me finish. I told you my parents helped me get a decent car and I was going to start driving out next month, but we need to see each other sooner than that. So this is what I'm going to do, I'm going to call the airlines right now to book a seat for next week. I know this is sudden but don't worry, I'll let Dave know I'm on my way, I won't just show up on your door step, I'll call him as soon as..." He was almost out of breath but still talking when she interrupted.

"Phillip, stop." No hesitancy in the command, and her voice was firm when she added "I don't think it's a good idea to rush out here. I need more time to talk to my parents. I haven't had a chance to sit down and tell them about us, I mean how serious it was between us."

He caught the word "was" but he let her continue.

"What I mean is, it's just been very busy around here. My mother is very involved with a summer program her church is sponsoring, and some days I don't see her till dinner time. Then, they've been talking about taking me on a vacation trip to Hawaii, it was a surprise graduation gift they'd been planning, and it could happen soon. My Dad is trying to work out his schedule..."

"Hawaii? Well, that does sound pretty great. How long do you think you'd be gone?" He took in a deep breath and felt better. That would explain why she'd been sounding so hesitant, caught up as she must have been in the uncertainty surrounding the trip.

65

"Oh, Phillip, how can I possibly know that? Don't do that, don't put pressure on me right now. I just told you I don't even know when we'd be going, much less how long we'd be gone."

He couldn't help thinking, despite her explanation, that surely in all those weeks there must have been some opportunity to grab enough time to talk to them, to let them know about her relationship with the man she loves. Didn't she owe them that much? And didn't she owe him at least that much? But he didn't say anything. Her last comment had been somewhat sharp, and he felt intimidated.

"Look," she said, breaking the silence, "All I'm trying to tell you is there is so much going on here that I need more time to think about everything. But right now I have to run because my parents just came home from shopping." Now she started talking much faster. "You just can't come out this soon, everything's up in the air right now. This is hard for me, please try to understand. I have to go. I love you, Phillip, really I do."

Hard for her? No, he didn't understand, and he started to respond but the click told him she was gone.

Yet another week went by, and the knot kept growing. Now it had gotten so big it was starting to interfere with swallowing. He was sure his parents must be wondering why he wasn't packing up and making plans for the drive. But they hadn't said anything about it, and he continued working at Tom's, glad for the distraction and the exhaustion at the end of his shift that let him fall asleep as soon as his head hit the pillow. He was trying hard to quell the turmoil in his mind, to keep fighting the feeling of dread that was growing stronger each day. He kept calling but it was getting harder to talk to her because her mother answered most of the time and would tell him very politely that Amanda wasn't there right now, that she would give her the message that he had called. But each time the lapse grew longer between calls. When he did manage to reach her, he could tell she was distancing herself more and more, offering vague responses and making excuses to get off the phone.

And then one hot, humid July morning, she called him, awakening him from a restless night's sleep. He'd worked the late shift the night before and hadn't gotten to bed until three. Feeling groggy, he looked at the clock as he picked up the phone. The sound of her voice startled him and wakened him instantly.

"Phillip? It's me, and we have to talk." Just like that, blunt and urgent, catching him off guard.

"Amanda, sweetheart," he managed to say, "you're up really early. It isn't even five where you are."

"I know. I couldn't sleep. I've been tossing and turning all night thinking about having to make this call."

He waited for what seemed long minutes before she spoke again.

"I can't do this any longer, Phillip. I would sooner cut off my right arm than do what I'm about to do to you. I need to tell you the truth about what's really going on with me. I'm so sorry to make you wait so long. God knows I haven't been fair to you."

It took a great effort to swallow before he could make his voice work.

"What... what are you talking about, Amanda? What truth? What is it that's going on with you?"

He heard her nervous throat-clearing. "There's no easy way to say this, Phillip, so I'll have to drop the bomb and get it over with. It's Brett. We're back together." Her words began speeding up, knocking against each other in her hurry to get them out. "His great love affair didn't work out, you see, and he says he's been thinking about me all this past year, waiting for me to come home, hoping I haven't found someone else. He says he's sorry it took him so long to wake up and realize he was a complete fool and that I'm the one and only love of his life. He wants to marry me, the sooner the better before he loses me again."

He tried to stay calm. "Did you tell him that you have fallen in love with someone else? Like, uh, me? And that you're going to marry me? The plan, Amanda, the plan, remember?" He waited a beat.

"I did try to tell him about you. About us. I did, Phillip, I swear it." She started to cry.

"What do you mean, you tried to tell him? Did you tell him or not?"

"I... I tried, I swear to God I tried, but he didn't want to hear it. Just like I know you won't want to hear this either, Phillip, but I have to say it anyway. After seeing him a few more times I could tell he really had changed. He really loves me. And I looked into my own heart and found I still cared about him. I ran from him, Phillip, and when I met you I guess I was still rebounding. I was so terribly hurt and I was still in so much pain. I wasn't being fair to you. I must have never really, truly fallen out of love with him, and…"

"Jesus, Amanda!" He could feel the rage now, it was pouring out of him like hot lava. "Is this what happens to people who are raised out there? Did living so close to Tinsel Town rub off on you that much?" He paused and she started to say something but he wouldn't let her speak.

"Well, congratulations on your acting job. You'd be a sure winner at the next Academy Awards if they have a category for best liar. You did one hell of a job on me. I fell for your garbage, and that's all it was, garbage. You had me convinced that you loved me and even jumped in with both feet to plan our future together, and now I see it was all one great big lie. How could you do that and still live with yourself?"

Now she was sobbing and he felt his heart turn over. He waited, trying to regain his composure. He had to think, fast and hard. Get hold of yourself, Phillip, calm down, you might still be able to salvage this.

"Look," he said, making a mighty effort to sound reasonable, "this is so out of the blue I can't make any sense of it sitting here in my room in Michigan, so far away from you. I'm sorry for what I just said to you, I love you so much and the last thing I meant to do was make you cry." Okay so far, so good. He was getting both his voice and his heart rate back to near normal. "We need to see each other, Amanda, and I don't give a damn if you don't want me to come out. I'm doing it. I have to. I'm hanging up the phone right this minute and calling for a seat on a plane today, tomorrow if I can't do it that fast. This time I'm not letting you talk me out of it. We can straighten this out, what we have is too precious to lose. That bastard Brett can go straight to hell if he thinks he's getting you back. He wants to marry you right away so he won't lose you again? He's lost you! He's not getting you back because I'm not letting you go, Amanda. You're not thinking straight, I'm the guy you love, remember?"

"It's too late. Too late." She barely got the words out, her voice hoarse with tears.

"What exactly does that mean? That you've slept with him? Amanda, tell me that didn't happen, not after…"

"Phillip! You must never, never forget I did love you. That was real, more real than anything…"

"Which is why I'm coming out as soon as I can."

"No, you can't. You just can't." He heard the deep indrawn breath before she delivered her next words.

"Yes, I did sleep with him, more than once. It just happened. He wants to marry me, he won't take no for an answer and my parents want me to marry him, they've known him for such a long time and they think I should give him another chance. I think they're right. You deserve to know the truth."

"The truth? What truth, Amanda!" The rage was back, full force. "How could you jump into bed with him right after...Oh, my God, how could you do that! Why did you lie to me, why did you keep lying to me all this time? Not having the time to tell them about us, all that dancing around, not returning my calls. Hawaii, was that another lie?"

"It's true, it's a gift, but not what I told you it was. It's going to be a wedding gift. A...a honeymoon."

The word exploded in his ear and left him speechless.

"I lied to you because I had to stop you from coming here, Phillip. I know you can never forgive me but I did love you so much. I still love you, you have to believe that." She had started to cry and now her sobs tore at his heart. "I'm sorry, Phillip. So, so sorry. You'll never know how much I..."

He slammed the phone into the cradle, then threw it across the room, over his bed, where it crashed to the floor and lay like a snake that might strike if he came close to it.

16

Approaching his driveway, Phillip's attention was caught by a bright pink hibiscus bush the landscapers had just planted in the corner of his small garden, so he didn't see Karla right away. Two mugs of coffee and a long walk had cleared his head of the cobwebs the pill had deposited there. He didn't like taking pills, but this time it was a price he willingly paid for eight hours of uninterrupted sleep. He had just started up the brick walkway that was shielded from his neighbor's by a dense hedge of night-blooming jasmine when he saw her. There she sat in the navy director's chair he kept on the front porch, pretty as a daffodil in a yellow lace-trimmed tennis dress. He stopped for a few seconds, then walked toward her, very slowly. She remained seated, her gaze inscrutable behind oversized sunglasses. Just like the redhead's, he thought for a fleeting second.

"Phillip?" A question followed by a slight pause. Then, "What the hell is going on?"

He didn't answer, couldn't. He was taken aback by her presence.

"What's the matter, cat got your tongue? Come on, Phillip. You called me two days ago and left a message. Then, let's see…"

She began ticking off the events on her fingers, one by one. "I returned your call the next day and asked you to call me. You didn't." Another finger. "I called you again, later. I waited to hear back from you last night, but you didn't call. Another finger. I thought surely I would hear from you this morning, but no, nothing. Were you out of town, Phillip? Or what? I'm here for one reason, and that's to find out why you're acting like this."

He found his voice. "I don't want to talk about it. And it would be better all the way around if you just left." He took out his key, opened the door. But she had sprung up quickly and followed him into the small foyer, closing the door behind her.

"Okay, let's have it. Tell me what's wrong. And no, it would not be better if I left. I'm not leaving before I find out what this is all about. I'm going to venture a wild guess that it has to do with my not getting back to you right away when I got your message. Am I right?"

He didn't say anything, and she walked past him into the living room and sat on the sofa.

"Oh, the silent treatment, is it? That isn't going to get us anywhere. All right, I'll play your game. Yes, Karla, I'm upset because you didn't call me back. Gee, I'm sorry, Phillip. I was busy and it was impossible to call you."

He couldn't stand it any longer. "Busy? I saw just how busy you were, Karla. I went down to Salty Sam's that night for a sandwich and a beer and…"

"You saw me? You saw me sitting there with a man and you, what, assumed it was a date? That I was, as they say, stepping out on you?"

"It most certainly did not look like a get-together with a casual acquaintance! Not from where I was sitting." Now he was angry, making no attempt to hide it. "And when you didn't bother to return my call that evening, why wouldn't I assume it was a date?" And, he added silently, I watched you drive back with him, disappear inside with him. He reddened at the memory. He could never, ever let her know he'd walked over to her building, sat in the gazebo all that time waiting for her to come home. And then stayed in the cold darkness until almost midnight, eyes fixed on the door watching for the guy who never came back out. And even worse, walking over there this morning to see if his car was still there. Spying on her, as though he had any business doing that, pathetic old fool that he was.

"Well, you're wrong. It was not a date. It was an emotionally exhausting day and evening and I'm going to tell you about it."

"No need," he replied quickly, waving his hand. He sat on the chair opposite her. "None of my business what you do, Karla, who you go out with. There are no strings in this relationship as far as I'm concerned."

"I hope you don't mean that, Phillip." Those beautiful blue eyes, damn her, focusing on him now with a seriousness he'd only rarely seen in them before. He tried looking away, to no avail. She had him.

"I thought we had something pretty special between us, and I was sure you did too. But anyway," raising her hand to silence him, "I'm going to tell you, whether or not you want to hear it. Listen to me and when I'm finished, I'll leave. I promise, cross my heart."

"Fine." He sighed, a deliberately exaggerated sigh. He knew it was childish, but didn't care.

"The man you saw me with was Caleb. My ex-husband, you might remember his name." He didn't nod but she continued "He showed up at my door two days ago around noon, just like that. Out of the blue, no phone call, nothing. I couldn't believe my eyes, but there stood Caleb, looking like his best friend just died. I'd never seen him like that. He just walked straight in as soon as I opened the door, and I was thinking what if someone was here with me, like you? But he looked so distraught, I believe the only thing on his mind was what had happened to him and he picked me to unload it on. He had never been here but of course he knew where I lived, where I had finally settled. And speaking of settling, you might remember my telling you Caleb was extremely generous where the financial aspect of our divorce was concerned. He happens to be a very wealthy man and nothing motivates generosity like good old-fashioned guilt."

He didn't comment but tried to look bored. He hated to admit it, but she'd hooked him. It hadn't occurred to him that the man could have been her ex-husband.

"I spent the rest of the day with him. Listening, mostly. Turns out that Cyndi, the sweet young thing he left me for, the mother of his children, left him and wants out of the marriage. Caleb doesn't understand the whole thing, but then he wouldn't. Apparently she isn't getting what she needs from him, whatever that is. And she's found it in the person of their son Timothy's Little League coach. Also rich, also married, I might add, but of course that wouldn't bother little Cyndi. After all, Caleb was married to me when she went after him. Or he went after her, I never did find out the finer points of that trashy little drama, nor would I be interested. I wish I could be a nicer person about the way it turned out, but part of me is actually not all that sorry that Caleb gets to find out how I felt when he left me for her."

She paused so long he felt he had to say something, but all he could come up with was "So?" And as soon as he said it, he knew he sounded like a petulant child.

"So," she repeated, an impatient emphasis on the word, "he's driving himself crazy wondering what he can do about it, and he felt he could come to me for advice. I didn't have any, Phillip, but that didn't keep him from talking and talking all day. Obviously, he was using me to vent. Anyway, it was getting close to dinner time so I suggested running down to Salty Sam's. I'd heard your message but I was in a hurry to get out of there, it was getting stifling being cooped up with him so long. I needed a break, or at least a change of scene." Pausing again, she looked at him. A long look, studying him.

"I need coffee, Phillip. Do you have some?"

He didn't, he'd drunk it all before his walk. "No," he said brusquely. Then, catching himself, he added in a slightly nicer tone "I guess I can make a fresh pot." He got up and headed for the kitchen, adding grudgingly "I could use some more too."

She drank half a mugful before she started talking again. "Thanks. You do make a good cup of coffee." He nodded, waiting, not smiling.

"When you saw us at the restaurant, he was still at it. We had a couple of drinks before we ordered food, but when it came, I don't think he ate half of it. He couldn't stop talking long enough to eat. I ate mine, though. I was hungry."

She was waiting for him to say something, so he thought he might as well tell her what had gone through his mind.

"I was trying not to be obvious when I looked at the two of you," he said. "At him, actually. You, or I should say what I could see of you, I recognized right away. I looked long enough, though, to be able to tell it seemed to be a very intense conversation."

"Yes, at that point it HAD gotten pretty intense. I think that was when he started apologizing for what he did to me all those years ago. I'm not sure if it was the start of an attempt to get back together or what, but he was going on about how I was his first love, how he'd never really forgotten me, how great it was to be talking to someone who'd known him a long time, who made him feel comfortable, someone who understood him…"

"He really used that tired old line? Did you manage to keep a straight face?"

"Yep. I didn't want to hurt him, he seemed like he was having a really bad time, and the fact is, I do understand him. A lot better now in retrospect than when I was married to him. Caleb has some problems, I think they're called issues these days, but I don't foresee spending any time pondering them at this stage of my life. I have much better things to do now and I don't want to expend energy analyzing Caleb the child, Caleb the grown-up, Caleb the unfaithful husband, and now Caleb the soon-to-be-ex-husband of an unfaithful wife."

"How did your evening end, then?" Phillip asked. "Did you spend more time with him after dinner, or did you send him on his way?"

"No, I didn't send him on his way." She sighed and set her mug on the table. "He wanted to come back up to my place and stay the night instead of trying to find a hotel room. He was so down, and he asked in a way that made me feel sorry for him, so I said okay." Another pause, another long look, this time with her eyes focused intently on his.

"And, Phillip, just in case you might be entertaining the tiniest notion of such a ridiculous possibility, I did not sleep with him. It happens that I sleep with no one but the man I have been sleeping with since one magical night in October, the one I'm in love with and the only one I ever want to sleep with. I am that old-fashioned creature, I think it's called a one-man woman." Phillip did not change his expression, and she continued talking. She was convincing, he'd give her that.

"I must give him credit for being smart enough to not even hint at that timeworn phrase 'how about just this once, honey, for old times' sake?' although I can't say for sure it didn't occur to him. Mainly, though, I think he just wanted to talk some more, and I let him even though I'd started to find it very draining to sit there listening all that time. But Phillip, Caleb is the past. There's nothing left of our time together. No children to bind us, even though I will always wish I could have had a child back then. But as you know so well, some things just aren't in the cards you've been dealt and you learn to live with that."

Phillip exhaled the breath he realized he'd kept holding, feeling the tension drain out of him. God help him, he believed her.

"So that's the story. I asked you to listen and you did, so now I'll leave just as I promised I would."

She set the empty mug on the table and started to get up, but he was there in a flash, lifting her to her feet, holding her, every electrifying inch of her pressed so close he felt himself going weak in the knees.

"Try it." He was murmuring huskily against silky hair that smelled like flowers washed by a rainstorm. "You in your sexy little tennis dress, just try leaving."

17

By the time they left the beach it was almost full dark and the main road on the Key sparkled with an endless chain of lighted decorations. Karla broke the silence in the car as they approached the bridge to the mainland. Reluctant to disturb the spell that surrounded them like a delicate web, she spoke very softly.

"That was beyond incredible. I never imagined spending Christmas Eve in a setting like that. The sunset was magnificent, the way that big orange ball disappeared into the Gulf and sent those gorgeous pink and gold and purple banners streaking across the sky."

He smiled and reached for her hand. "Yes, it was. And you just painted a perfect picture with your words."

"I want to do this every year, Phillip. I was mesmerized. Everyone was. I heard just one comment, a woman saying that all we needed to make it perfect was seeing the green flash. What did she mean?"

"I heard it too. The green flash is defined technically as atmospheric dispersion and also as astronomical refraction. Makes your head spin reading about it. To me it's a meteorological phenomenon. It appears on the horizon in that microsecond just when it looks as though the sun is dropping right into the water. It is seen by the human eye only rarely, and it happens so swiftly that if you blink you miss it."

"Have you ever seen it?"

"Yes, and just once, years ago. We were vacationing at a place south of here and happened to be on the beach right at the critical moment. I remember how excited all the sunset watchers around us were that day. It really is something special. There are some who swear it is nothing but baloney, bogus. But for those of us who have actually seen it, we know differently. It happens but as I said, it's seen rarely. Others even view it as a sign that something miraculous is happening, or is about to happen. Maybe you and I will see it someday, if we're lucky."

Absorbing what he had just told her, Karla was silent for a few moments before she spoke again.

"Okay, another question. How did you find out about that little church across the road from the beach offering such a beautiful way to celebrate Christmas Eve?"

"Actually, it was Claudia who discovered it when we moved here. I think one of our neighbors mentioned it to her a few weeks before Christmas. It isn't just for parishioners, everyone is welcome. This evening the crowd was bigger than I've ever seen it. When we saw it that first time we were so impressed, I remember we thought about joining that church, but we never followed through."

"But did you come here every year after that?"

"Yes. Twice a year, actually. At sunrise on Easter Sunday too, which is every bit as glorious as tonight's sunset ceremony." He cleared his throat before he added "I must admit, though, I didn't attend either service after Claudia died. It was just too painful."

"I think I can understand that. Divorce is much different, of course, but there were things I used to do with Caleb that I no longer wanted to do by myself or even with June. Like eating at the restaurant we went to a lot when we were dating, a small, out-of-the-way place where the owner practically adopted us and made sure we got very special attention. Things like that can bring back some pretty hurtful memories." She sighed. "I don't mean to make comparisons, Phillip. It's just that divorce is, well, a kind of death, in its own way."

He tightened his grip on her soft hand.

"I've heard that said before, and I'm so sorry, Karla." There was a small pause, and when he spoke again his voice changed, became upbeat. "I have an idea. Beginning this very evening, let's start our own tradition, make new memories. Like having dinner at Something's Fishy after the service every Christmas Eve from now on.

Okay with you?"

At once the atmosphere in the car lightened, and she smiled.

"More than okay. Where we had our first date! I love it. Let's go!"

They exchanged gifts after breakfast on Christmas morning. Karla had created a cozy holiday atmosphere with logs glowing in the fireplace and a gaily decorated fresh fir filling the room with the pungent fragrance of the north woods.

He opened his gift first, at her insistence. A handsome wood frame held a numbered print signed by the artist, a woman of considerable renown who lived in a village in the northern part of Michigan's Lower Peninsula. The original, according to the small printed enclosure, had been hung in the Toledo Museum of Art. The painting portrayed a forest in autumn, the colors soft on an overcast day, a doe and her fawn in the foreground. Karla had spotted it months before in one of the downtown galleries and knew at once that it was perfect for the man who spoke wistfully and often of autumn in Michigan. Now his gasp of genuine surprised delight, and the catch in his voice as he thanked her were all the affirmation she could wish for.

Her turn. Browsing in one of the shops that lined Antique Alley, Phillip had spotted a beautiful necklace. The owner told him it was part of a collection of fine jewelry acquired from the estate of a prominent New York television executive who had lived in a local retirement community until his death a few months ago. Phillip's eye was drawn immediately to the topaz flanked by two small diamonds in the center of the intricately crafted silver chain. The gemstone was exactly the same shade of blue as Karla's eyes, and as soon as he saw it he envisioned the way it would look on the skin just beneath her throat. And now, when he heard her sharp intake of breath as she lifted the lid of the small purple box, he knew it had been a lucky find. She stared at him, eyes swimming, and it took a moment before she was able to thank him. Then she stood and handed him the necklace, asking him to help with the clasp. When she turned to face him, he placed his hands on her shoulders and stepped back to gaze at her.

"You are a beautiful woman," he said softly, "and I was right about the topaz. It really is the same color as your eyes."

They ate dinner on the balcony. A thin mist veiled the setting sun, lending an ethereal glow to the atmosphere. Karla had roasted a small goose, a tradition incorporating her great-great-grandmother's dressing recipe. They agreed to forego cocktails in favor of the outrageously expensive French champagne Phillip brought, and they savored each golden drop to the very end of their first Christmas dinner together.

18

Phillip was deep in thought as he strolled at a leisurely pace on this warm breezy morning after Christmas, barely noticing holiday decorations; wreaths, trees and bushes strung with lights now reflecting the sun, an occasional reindeer guarding a walkway. His mind was filled with new memories. Sunset on the beach just two evenings ago, and the start of their own tradition of Christmas Eve dinner at Something's Fishy. Yesterday and last night already had assumed the quality of a dream, beginning with breakfast and the exchange of those impossibly perfect gifts. Even now he could taste the champagne they shared all throughout the memorable dinner on the balcony that was made even more enchanting by the luminescence surrounding them. Perhaps best of all was waking up this morning to the sight of his sleeping lover wearing nothing but the necklace she had refused to take off when they went to bed last night. Bright sunlight was beaming through the louvers they hadn't bothered to close, caught the topaz and reflected it on the ceiling in a shower of tiny sparkling fragments, millions of them, in every color of the rainbow.

On the sidewalk just ahead a little girl was riding a pink bicycle with training wheels attached, under the watchful eye of a woman who waved at him. He waved back, trying to recall her last name. Marlene something, a nice woman enjoying her visiting granddaughter. The little girl greeted him as he approached, a pretty child with huge brown eyes.

"Santa brought me this!" she declared, and he noticed the bicycle was decorated with colorful strips of tinsel that glittered in the sun.

"What a beautiful bike!" he said. "You must have been a very good girl."

"I was! I ate all my vegetables and helped my Mommy take the dishes off the table after dinner. And I made up with Patty after our fight, even though I didn't really want to. Did Santa bring you something you wanted?"

"Oh yes he did." And so much more than I ever could have dreamed of, Phillip thought as he waved and walked on.

The sight triggered a memory of the Christmas when he got his first bicycle. So long ago, but he remembered it even though he hadn't yet turned five. It started on Thanksgiving night when Gordon brought up the subject of Santa Claus. They were sharing Phillip's room while their grandparents, visiting for the holiday, occupied Gordon's more spacious one. Phillip was on the verge of falling asleep when he heard his brother's voice in the darkness.

"Do you believe in Santa Claus, Phillip?"

"Yes. I think I do, anyway." Lately, though, he'd been wondering about just that. His best friend Walter had planted doubts in his mind on the way home from kindergarten a couple of weeks ago, bragging that he knew there wasn't any Santa Claus and if you still believed that, you had to be a baby.

"Why did you ask me that, Gordy?"

"Oh, no reason. Go to sleep, sorry if I woke you up."

On Christmas Eve that year, Phillip lay wide awake in his bed for a very long time, unable to fall asleep. As usual, his mother had handed him a glass of milk and a couple of cookies, directing him to put them on the hearth so Santa could have his snack when he came down the chimney. By then he was pretty sure the whole thing was a made-up story like the tooth fairy but he knew that for some reason his parents wanted him to still believe it was true. It must have been very late when he tiptoed out of his bed and came part of the way downstairs. He stopped when he heard voices in the living room. He heard his mother ask his father if he needed her help. He seemed to be putting something together because he asked her to hand him a wrench from his toolbox. Right then a small voice in his head told him to go back to his bed, now.

The next morning he ran down the stairs, looked into the living room, and knew for sure that there was no Santa Claus. And the thing was, it didn't make him the least bit sad. He was far too excited, seeing the shiny bright blue two-wheeler, a brand new one, not a hand-me-down from Gordon. Of course that was what his father was working on last night, attaching the training wheels.

It must have been very early because it was still dark outside and he was the only one awake. He went back to bed full of excitement and pretended to be asleep when his mother came into his room. She took him downstairs and made him close his eyes as they approached the living room. When she told him to open them, he clapped his hands and ran to the bicycle, shouting "Oh boy! Look what Santa brought me! Just what I wanted!" By then, his father and Gordon were there, Gordon hanging back in the doorway. When he caught Phillip's eye, Phillip could tell that he knew he was putting on a show for the benefit of their mother and father. It was like a secret between them, and that gave him the feeling of having grown up a lot just since Thanksgiving. He believed that now he was much closer to being on the same level as his adored big brother.

19

It was nice, having the pool all to themselves. Karla had called earlier, suggesting a swim after lunch, but Phillip was looking into road repair estimates and begged off. He'd barely taken time for a sandwich because he had decisions to make for next week's board meeting. The thought of a dip in the temperate water kept surfacing in his brain, though, and he called her a few hours later. He hadn't come to all the necessary conclusions yet, but business could wait

"I've been thinking about that swim. It does sound appealing. How about making it a sunset watch too? It's pretty quiet around that time. Then maybe a bite to eat at Sam's?"

"Sounds great. Meet you at the pool when, maybe a little after five?"

"Perfect."

After swimming leisurely laps, they stood leaning against the edge at the shallow end and watched the setting sun paint the clouds above the Gulf in constantly changing hues.

"It must be beautiful over on the beach right now." Karla sighed. "This is still so new to me, you know. My first winter here, and I can't quite believe I'm outdoors in a swimming pool in January! I've never been in Florida at this time of year. It was always in the spring or early summer, never right now when people back in Indiana are still recovering from the holidays."

"Yeah, the hangovers and overeating, and…" He was interrupted by a splash at the deep end, and they both turned to look. A swimmer wearing goggles surfaced, and even in the deepening twilight they could tell it was the redhead with the pony tail. They watched as she began swimming laps with smooth, perfectly synchronized strokes.

"Well, look who's here, you lucky duck. Your girlfriend! And she's quite a swimmer, it appears. Want to watch for a while?" She jabbed him with her elbow.

"Of course I do," he laughed, grabbing her arm and holding it firmly, "but darn it, I promised you something to eat at Sam's. We should be going. I'll take a quick shower and change, then I'll pick you up."

She stopped when they reached the street and brought her hand to her mouth to cover a yawn.

"You know, I've just changed my mind about dinner. I think I'll skip it for tonight. I really ran around that court this morning and I guess being in the water is what's made me feel relaxed and sleepy all of a sudden. The idea of a warm bath and taking my new book to bed sounds irresistible. But thanks for the invitation anyway." A quick kiss, and they parted.

After a long shower Phillip finished the task he had laid aside earlier, then made himself a Manhattan. He looked forward to a pleasant evening catching up on the news on his favorite channel, a simple dinner of various leftovers that actually looked appealing and finally, a chance to watch a Michigan State basketball game. On the home court, no less, a real thrill for a lifetime Spartan fan. Perfect. He settled in his chair and took the first satisfying sip. And heard the doorbell.

Aha, he thought, she changed her mind again. Well, fine. He could change his plan too, and happily. She'd like a glass of the Pinot he picked up last week at the wine shop that just opened across from the shopping center, and then they'd run down to Sam's for a light dinner. He clicked off the TV and smiled as he walked to the door.

Only it wasn't Karla standing there. It took a second to register that here stood the redhead, wearing a white sundress. No ponytail tonight, her hair lay in a thick wavy mass down past her shoulders. And no sunglasses, so he could see all of a very pretty face.

"Excuse me, but you are Phillip Ashcroft, right?"

It seemed to take a long moment before he could find his voice.

"Yes, I'm Phillip Ashcroft. Won't you come in, please?" He stepped aside and she took a few tentative steps into the living room. What in heaven's name was she doing here?

"This is really awkward," she said with an apologetic smile, "I mean, I know your name, obviously, but you don't know mine. Anyway, I'm Madeline Schuster and you and I pass each other walking all the time and you have to be wondering why I'm here on your doorstep." Clearly, she was nervous.

"Yes, I admit I'm a little curious. And surprised. But it's a pleasure to see you, Miss Schuster, or is it…"

"Well, I'm divorced and officially I'm a 'Ms.', I guess. As I just told you, my name is Madeline but everyone calls me Maddie. I'd like it if you would call me Maddie even though you don't know me."

"Okay, Maddie, and now that you've introduced yourself, I'd like you to call me Phillip." He was over his initial shock and now he was simply wondering what had brought her here. His first thought, though, was to try to put this young woman at ease.

"I was just about to indulge in my nightly cocktail, as you can see, and I'd like to offer you a drink. Maybe a glass of wine?"

"Oh, I interrupted," she said, accepting his gesture to sit on the sofa, "You are so nice to offer a drink to a stranger, and yes, I'd like whatever wine you have handy. I guess you can tell I'm nervous, but I promise I'm not going to try to sell you anything." Pause. "And I'll explain why I just showed up out of nowhere."

"I'll listen to whatever you have to say, Maddie. And please try not to be nervous. It isn't every day an old guy like me gets an unexpected visit from an attractive young lady."

Opening the wine bottle, Phillip had a chance to think about the way she looked without those big glasses. She resembled someone, but who? And why did her eyes strike a chord in his memory? Amber eyes rimmed with green, tilted slightly up at the corners.

"This is very good," she commented after the first sip. "And," noting his scrutiny, "I don't blame you for sizing me up. But you look as though I remind you of someone. Am I right?"

"You are, and forgive my rudeness for staring. I was trying to think of who you look like. Maybe someone in the movies? Or on TV?"

"Or from your past." Her look became suddenly serious. "Amanda Stewart? I don't look exactly like her, although quite often people do see a resemblance. I'm her daughter."

"Oh, my God! Amanda." It caught in his throat, came out just barely above a whisper. His hand shook, and he tightened his grip on the glass he was holding.

"Are you okay? You're very pale. I'm sorry, Phillip. I shouldn't have blurted it out like that."

"No, I'm all right." He placed his hand over his heart and tried a smile. "I won't have a heart attack, I promise."

"I did that badly," she said, taking a long sip of wine, "and I really am sorry. It's just that it's taken me a long time to get up enough nerve to introduce myself. I kept waiting for the right opportunity but…well, tonight I left the pool right after you and your companion did, and when I saw you walking toward your place by yourself, I decided to take a chance. I ran home, got dressed and drove here before I completely lost my nerve. I didn't mean to scare you."

He smiled and took another sip. "You didn't really, you just surprised me. I thought you were Karla – my companion, as you call her – and that she had changed her mind about my dinner invitation. Speaking of which, I was planning to fix a plate of leftovers for myself. Nothing great, but there's enough for two if you haven't eaten yet. What do you say? And then, when my stomach isn't growling, you can tell me all about yourself and why you came to see me."

"As a matter of fact, I haven't had dinner yet. And I sure didn't plan to come here and have a dinner offer, but what the heck! I love leftovers." Now she smiled, looking relaxed and oddly at home. "Can I do anything?"

"Nope." He was feeling at ease with this young woman. He liked her, this daughter of Amanda's.

"You know," he said, studying her face as they ate, "I should have seen the resemblance at once, because it is definitely there. Before tonight I never got a good look at your face."

"I know," she smiled, "it's those sunglasses. Some of my friends tease me about hiding behind them because they're bigger than most. Celebrities out shopping in L.A. always wear them, of course, although I've always had this suspicion that some of the lesser-known ones might get miffed if they're not recognized. You've been in L.A., I'm sure."

"Yes, my late wife Claudia and I spent quite a bit of time on the west coast, especially during the winter months. There, and here in Florida whenever we could get away."

"I've heard about Michigan winters. And I have to say that although I love snow for skiing in the mountains, dealing with it daily would be another matter. Look, I know it's taking me forever to tell you why I'm here, but before I start, may I have a little more of this nice wine?"

He refilled her glass and joined her with a glass of his own, guessing he would need it. Her coming here had to be about Amanda. And it was, of course.

She'd decided to look him up, she explained, after learning from her mother about their relationship all those years ago in college. A year and a half ago her father, Brett Caldwell, an apparently healthy man, had suffered an aneurism of the brain while playing golf. It can happen with absolutely no warning, she told him, and is almost always fatal. He died almost immediately. They were all traumatized – her mother, her two brothers, herself.

"How awful," Phillip interrupted, "and I can empathize because I had a similar experience, sadly. My wife died suddenly, too, with no prior symptoms. She had a stroke. It occurred while she slept, and it was too late to save her when I found her. She was alive, but barely, and the second stroke, the fatal one, hit on the way to the hospital. But please go on. I'm so sorry for your loss, Maddie."

"Thank you. Phillip. So you got hit with the same double whammy, death and shock. I'm so sorry. I know from being with my mother how terrible it is to lose a spouse that way."

"And you and your brothers…to lose a beloved parent so suddenly and cruelly. Claudia and I were childless and…"

"That meant you had nobody to turn to, right? My mother had us and we all took comfort in mourning our loss together, but you had no one…although come to think of it, I do remember that when she told me about you, she mentioned you had a brother, an older one."

He nodded in reply without comment, not wishing to discuss Gordon and their relationship right now. More than enough was going on tonight as it was. It occurred to him that this evening had evolved into something far removed from what he had anticipated an hour or so ago. Surreal, he decided, that would describe it. When she realized he wasn't going to say anything more, she broke the momentary silence.

"Okay, about why I'm here tonight. To cut right to it, Phillip, my mother is in a very bad way and I looked you up because I had this hope that maybe you could help her. And me, and my brothers as well.

It has to do with what happened between you all those years ago. But feel free to stop me if you don't want me to dredge up old stuff you'd prefer not to hear. You can tell me if this is too much of an intrusion, and I'll just finish my wine, tell you it was nice to meet you because it really was, and leave you in peace."

"That isn't going to happen, Maddie. This is not an intrusion, and you must tell me all about it now that you've come this far. I have nothing but time this evening. Your mother and I were very close once, and it distresses me to learn that things aren't well with her. Of course I'd like to help if you think I can." It was true. At the moment all the old animosity toward Amanda had vanished and his immediate concern was for this young woman whose earlier anxiety seemed to have returned, who was looking ready to bolt if he couldn't convince her he wanted her to stay.

"Well, first of all," she began, "she's financially secure. Daddy was a good provider and always planned for their future. It's her emotional state we're concerned about. She seemed to recover afterward, at least for a short while, but gradually we started to notice signs of worsening depression. She started turning down invitations to lunch with old friends and became withdrawn and quiet. Too quiet, which isn't like her. For one overlong stretch, I couldn't even get her to go out with me for lunch and shopping, things both of us always loved to do together. My brothers and I offered to find her a grief counselor or at least one of those groups of widowed people who meet on a regular basis to talk and share experiences and lend each other support and encouragement. She turned us down, politely, insisting she didn't need it."

"Not unusual. I was offered that kind of therapy by a good, well-meaning doctor but I too declined. Looking back, I guess it might have made things easier but…anyway, go on."

"Both my brothers are married, both with children, and of course very busy. Dana is a dentist and Daniel is a graphic artist. They do their best, and so do their wives, to give as much attention to our mother as possible, but it's easier for me to spend more time with her. I'm a freelance writer for a couple of trade magazines, so I can basically arrange my own schedule. Anyway, I became aware sooner than they did that something was very wrong. Call it female intuition or the special bond between mother and daughter. They thought she was adjusting slowly to widowhood, and at first I did too, but as time went on I began to worry. By being persistent – you might call it nagging -- I did eventually get her to start coming to my place for an occasional dinner, or lunch at her favorite seafood restaurant in Santa Monica. That's where we were, looking out the window at the ocean across the street, when I realized she was feeling especially anxious that day. She even had a second glass of wine, which she almost never does. I kept encouraging her to tell me what was on her mind, and that was when she told me all about you, Phillip, and what happened back then."

He picked up the glass he had set on the coffee table and took a long swallow. "Did she tell you...everything?" He realized he was holding his breath, and exhaled slowly.

"If you mean, well, the nitty-gritty, the personal stuff, of course not. My Mom is not like that. From what she told me, I gathered that Daddy was her first love from way back in high school, but he had some crazy fling cheating on her one summer and she went tearing off to Michigan, where she met you and you fell in love with each other. His affair with the other woman apparently ended disastrously. He told her he dated different women in college after that, but finally realized Mom was his true love. Only she wasn't there, she was in Michigan, and wouldn't take his phone calls or answer his letters. So he started pleading his case to my grandparents. He must have been a terrific salesman, because they ended up believing he really loved her and truly regretted what happened. The two mothers were very close friends, so there were family pressures in the mix. The upshot was, when she flew home after graduating, my grandmother told her about Daddy almost as soon as her plane landed. They didn't know she was in love with you, so I guess both of them felt free to encourage her to give him another chance, since they were convinced he deserved it. That was the start of their getting back together." She paused to take a sip of her wine. "I guess you could say that was it, they reconciled, married and lived happily ever after. Except for this one thing that has emerged after all this time. She told me she has never made peace with herself over the way she ended things with you."

Nor, he thought, have I ever found peace with it, the question that never has stopped haunting me. But he said nothing.

"I'm taking forever to get to the point of my visit, Phillip, but here it is: I believe that after all those years of suppressing her guilt about the way she treated you, losing Daddy played a part in bringing it back. Do you know what I mean? The guilt on top of the normal grief adding up to a double dose of depression. You know, geriatrics has always interested me, and I've done some research in my spare time. One thing I've learned is that very often people, as they age, tend to dwell a lot on things that happened in the past, sometimes to the point of obsessing about them. And that's what I think is happening to her. Just my theory, and I'm not a psychologist, but I believe she's tormenting herself over the way she broke your heart."

"And she did exactly that, Maddie. I have to be completely honest with you just as you've been with me, and tell you I didn't think I could ever be whole again. My world had crashed at twenty-three. But as in all things, time was the great healer. She found happiness in marriage, as it turned out, and so did I. Eventually." He looked at his empty glass and saw that hers was empty too.

"Would you like more wine or perhaps coffee? I have the real thing or decaf if you'd prefer that. Either way, I was told by Karla just recently that I make a great pot of coffee."

"I would love coffee, thank you. The real thing. I need it. I'm about to ask a tremendous favor of you."

She waited until the hot, fragrant coffee was poured into mugs and each had taken a few sips before she spoke again.

"I don't want to spend any more time getting to the point of this visit, which I think is pretty bizarre and I can't believe you are being so calm and nice about having a stranger just pop in out of nowhere. And listening to her. But anyway, it's taking more courage than I ever would have thought I possessed to ask this of you, but is there any possible way you could fly to L.A. with me to visit my mother? So she could see you, talk to you, and hopefully ease her conscience, finally. This is my idea, not hers, I want you to know. She would be appalled if she knew what I was doing. She thinks I came here because of a project I'm doing for one of the publications I work for. That's partly true, I am doing some work while I'm here, but finding you was my real reason for coming here. She has no idea where you are. She doesn't know anything about you, if you're married or even if you're still alive. What she told me that day at lunch was how much she wished she could tell you what happened, but that she feels you would not have any interest since it is ancient history now. But you see, Phillip, I've taken it upon myself to try to do just that, see if being able to talk to you would relieve her of an enormous and I believe debilitating burden."

He started to speak but she interrupted. "The thing is, besides the normal aging you'd expect, there's been a significant difference in how she looks. I might be worrying needlessly, it probably has a lot to do with grieving. She is thinner than I've ever known her to be, still beautiful but...sometimes I wonder if she isn't keeping something from me. She never lets me take her when she goes to the doctor's for checkups and I can't bring myself to try to find out if something is going on because she is a very private person. If I mention anything about her health she says she's just getting older and tires more easily'"

She took a long sip of coffee and set her mug on the table. Looking at him squarely, she continued "If you could find it in your heart to come with me to visit her, I would be forever in your debt. Of course I would insist on covering all expenses because I know this is an outrageous request and part of me can't believe I'm actually making it…"

There was a long silence as her voice trailed off. She was asking a lot, and he took some time before answering.

"It isn't outrageous, Maddie. It's a plea from a daughter who cares deeply about her troubled mother. I will think about it, but of course I would not allow you to cover any expenses if I do agree to go. Give me a day or two."

But he knew he would not have to think about it. He would go, and he knew it as soon as she made her request. He'd always wanted to know what really happened, why she had betrayed him, and now the opportunity awaited him. He would listen to her explanation, probe for every hidden detail, and maybe at last be able to put that ghost to rest. Besides, Maddie had been so earnest making her appeal for his help that he felt hard put to turn her down. First, though, he'd talk it over with Karla and give her a chance to air her thoughts about it.

20

He was deep in a dream about shoveling the driveway in Michigan after a snow storm when he was awakened by a persistent ringing. He surfaced gradually, reached for the phone on the night stand, and answered in a voice thick with sleep. It was Karla, laughing.

"Well, good morning, sleepyhead. Rough night?"

"Yeah, you could say that." Glancing at the clock, he saw it was eight-thirty. He shook his head, trying to clear it, and pulled up the sheet and light blanket he'd kicked off during the restless night. No wonder he was dreaming about snow, he'd felt chilled.

"Oh? Were you with another woman, you dog?"

"As a matter of fact, I was." Now he was fully awake, remembering. "I can't talk about it right now. I have a lot to tell you about last night and I need your input, but I have to think about it first. I've got to get some caffeine into my veins, and then I'll go for a walk and call you when I get back. My brain is in need of coffee and fresh air."

Home again, he poured another mug from the carafe and feeling more clear-headed, called Karla.

"I've been waiting for your call," she said, "and I'm dying to know what's going on. You're not leaving me for that other woman, are you?"

"Sorry, lady, you're stuck with me, like it or not. Seriously, though, I do need to talk to you. Something very…well, interesting, to say the least, has come up and I'd like your take on it. Are you free for lunch?"

"Are you kidding? I can't wait for lunch. Come over right now, it's still early and I'll fix breakfast."

"Sounds great. I'm starving."

Clouds had moved in from the Gulf, obscuring the sun. It was cool but pleasant on the balcony, and he told her about last night's visit from Maddie as they ate crisp bacon, eggs and tomato slices that actually tasted like the ones Claudia had tended all those Michigan summers in their small garden. Toasted English muffins and his favorite cherry Danish rested on a warm platter. She listened intently, absorbing the details of what Maddie had related and what she had asked of him. It was almost noon when they finished, and a sudden sharp breeze ruffled the paper napkins on the table. They went inside to finish their coffee, and for a time a silence lay between them. Karla spoke first, asking him if he was thinking of agreeing to make the trip.

"I'm considering it. The whole thing, as you can imagine, interfered with my beauty sleep last night." She smiled, and he added "I'm leaning toward saying yes, and I'd be interested in what you think, Karla. Take your time. It was a lot for me to process and here I am dumping it on you. But I really would appreciate it if you'd give it some thought, then call me and let me know. I asked her to give me a day or two."

There was a long pause before she said "I don't need to think about it, Phillip, because I sense that you believe it's the right thing to do. I happen to think so too, and I'll tell you why." She reached for his hand.

"Isn't it strange, the things life can throw in our path with absolutely no forewarning?" Shaking her head, she continued, "Like the way it turns out that the pony-tailed redhead you mentioned noticing on your walks, the one we saw at the pool last evening, just happens to be the daughter of your first great love at Michigan State." She shook her head, musing. "Whoever would have guessed it? This Maddie must be a very special young woman to be so concerned about her mother that she was willing to take this kind of risk. I think you said she told you that she looked you up. She must have done a great deal of detective work to find you. And when you think about it, she couldn't have known what to expect when she did, what sort of person she would encounter. You could have turned out to be a cold, unforgiving man who refused to listen to her." She looked at him, a long, loving look. "But you're not. You're my dearest, most wonderful Phillip, and Maddie lucked out. As I did, having you come into my life."

"I'm the lucky one, Karla, for more reasons than I can count. Now I have to add to that long list your being so incredibly understanding." He had expected her to encourage him to grant Maddie's request, and she had not disappointed him. He kissed her and headed for the door, saying "I think I'll go home and spend some more time sorting things out in my head, which you've helped clear of cobwebs. Thank you, darling."

She stood outside the open door watching him and blew a kiss as he turned to wave before stepping into the elevator. She remained there for a long moment after he had disappeared, reflecting. He had asked for her input, and she had tried to respond honestly. She loved him so, and believed with all her heart that he loved her. There was not a scintilla of doubt that she could trust the strength of that love, and yet it was hard to ignore that little frisson of anxiety that had arisen with the news that he was considering going to Los Angeles to meet with Amanda. Amanda, his first love, Amanda who had broken his young heart, Amanda who was widowed and yes, available. Yet she had encouraged him to go and now there was no turning back.

Heading for the balcony to clear the table, she paused in the living room and reached for his coffee mug. Closing her eyes, she held her lips against the rim. It was still warm where his mouth had been.

Karla had insisted on driving them to the airport and when the two women were introduced, it was immediately apparent they liked each other. Not surprising, Phillip thought. Karla had expressed admiration for the courage Maddie exhibited in approaching him for the sake of her mother's well-being, and Maddie was pleased to learn that Karla had encouraged him to make the trip.

Maddie wanted him to take the window seat so that he could enjoy the view from thirty thousand feet on this sunny afternoon. She told him she was familiar with it, having flown several times between California and Florida for client meetings in Tampa, and once for a convention in Orlando. And indeed Phillip was mesmerized by the sight below, the Gulf a beautiful green where it met the seemingly endless stretch of white sand. He and Claudia always flew out of Michigan, so he found this new route fascinating. Soon, he knew, they would fly above bayous and the Mississippi, over plains and prairies, over desert and foothills. Then the magnificent mountains and finally the blue grandeur of the Pacific as the plane prepared to land in Los Angeles.

"It is different, isn't it, from the landscape you fly over when you leave the Midwest." She seemed to be reading his thoughts. "I remember that you told me how you and your wife would seek an occasional reprieve from Michigan winters by taking off for either Florida or southern California. That route would have taken you over the Grand Canyon, I believe."

He nodded. "Yes, and I never tired of looking down at the grandeur below. And now this, a magnificent vista new to me. Maddie, we are so blessed, aren't we, to live in this country?" She smiled, nodding, and laid her hand on his. She had told him flying made her sleepy, and as soon as the seatbelt sign disappeared, she yawned and closed her eyes. She put her seatback into in the reclining position and was asleep almost immediately. Her head was resting against his right shoulder, and he adjusted his seat to match hers. He remembered how Claudia never slept on a plane, always looking out the window or turning on the overhead light and reading when it was dark outside. Another memory of Claudia, another reminder that she was taken from him much too soon. He closed his eyes and saw her face, not the lifeless one he kissed and bade farewell at the hospital two years ago, but the face he had seen for the first time one beautiful spring afternoon almost thirty-five years ago. Maddie was fast asleep now and he found himself drifting into a reverie of remembering.

21

Western Michigan had been blessed with a string of warm, almost balmy days, rare for early April, when Phillip Ashcroft met Claudia Chamberlin for the first time. It was a day so fine, he walked the mile and a half from his office to drop off a contract at the law firm of Appleby and Scott for Bob Appleby's final approval. He was prepared to tease a smile from Bob's all-business, no-nonsense legal secretary and receptionist, Gertrude Carter, a task he enjoyed. His private name for the elderly woman with long white wavy hair was Gravel Gertie, borrowed from an old comic strip he'd read as a child. Unlike the friendly cartoon character who made him chuckle, Gertrude smiled infrequently, and that made the challenge all the more intriguing. He'd decided on one of his corny greetings, something like "How is my favorite glamour girl this lovely spring day?" but stopped short as he approached the glass door. Gravel Gertie was nowhere to be seen. In her chair sat a very pretty young woman with stylishly cut shiny dark hair, who looked at him appraisingly with intelligent blue-gray eyes as he stepped inside, then stood and offered her hand.

"Hi, I'm Claudia Chamberlin, Mr. Appleby's new assistant. You must be Phillip Ashcroft. The receptionist at your office phoned to let us know you were on your way with a contract."

He was tongue-tied for an instant as he shook her hand, staring at her.

"You look surprised, Mr. Ashcroft, which is understandable. Miss Carter left a month ago. Anyway, it's nice to meet you."

"It's my pleasure, Miss Chamberlin." He had quickly noted that the ring finger of her left hand was perfectly bare.

She started to speak but was interrupted by Bob Appleby's hearty greeting as he walked into the room.

"Phillip! By God, it's been ages since you honored us with your presence. You're looking great! I see you've met the newest addition to our little family here, Miss Claudia." He smiled and draped an arm over Phillip's shoulder. "Come on into my office, I'd enjoy a little chat with you unless you're in a hurry."

"Of course, Bob. I'd like that. Never too busy to talk to you." He handed the envelope to the attorney and followed him into the spacious office that smelled of books and a hint of cigar smoke. He made himself comfortable on the leather sofa and waved his hand to refuse the cigar Bob was offering, watching the older man light the one he'd chosen from a silver humidor. They discussed current happenings in the city, and Phillip remembered hearing about the attorney's participation in the recent rezoning matter.

"I heard you were asked to address a couple of points that hadn't shown up in previous agreements, Bob, even though John Decker is a commissioner."

"Yes, and a fine lawyer, but each of us has his own little corner of expertise when it comes to certain areas of the law, Phillip." He took a deep draft on the cigar, set it aside and asked "So, what did you think when you walked in the door and there sat Miss Chamberlin front and center? Surprised?"

"Yes, I must admit I was. I had no idea Gertrude was thinking of retiring. She struck me as a woman who would stay as long as she could manage to get here every morning and sit up straight in her chair. I'm going to miss trying to break through that wall of hers and getting a smile once in a blue moon. There was one time I almost heard the start of a chuckle, believe it or not."

"Oh, you had a way with her, Phillip. I know that because when you were expected she kind of brightened up. She didn't want to retire," he continued, his expression serious, "and she's in good health, as far as I know. But she has a father in his 90s down in Lafayette who has been in bad shape for going on ten years, and her brother has been his caretaker. Now he, the brother, has been diagnosed with a terminal cancer and can't do it anymore, so Gertrude has had to take over. She won't be back anytime soon. Meanwhile," he said, his smile back, "what do you think of our Claudia? Quite a looker, isn't she?"

"She is very pretty, Bob, but I'm sure you didn't hire her just to decorate the office, knowing you."

"Maybe you don't know me, son. Just kidding," he chuckled. Taking another deep draft of the cigar, he added "She's very bright, has the training and some experience. Not to put down dear Gertrude, but in all honesty I'd have to say Claudia seems to be on her way to being even better as far as efficiency is concerned. She learns fast and she's very competent. A couple of times, in fact, she has even pointed out little mistakes I missed. It's lucky for me that she moved here."

"Oh, so she's new here. I didn't think I'd seen her around town. Where is she from?"

"Dearborn. She moved here a couple of months ago to help her uncle, her late father's brother, look after his wife, who has Parkinson's. They're her only family except for an aunt in Los Angeles and some cousins out there. About a year ago, her parents were killed in a head-on collision one night coming home from an anniversary celebration in Grosse Pointe. The case is still being adjudicated, there are ongoing questions about culpability. Anyway, Phillip, I have to admit I've been wanting you two to meet. If I was a handsome young buck like you and met this lovely girl who incidentally is not wearing a ring, as you would have noticed if you're as sharp as I think you are…"

"What is this, Bob? Your new part-time job, moonlighting as Cupid?"

Grinning, Bob glanced at his watch and stood, which Phillip took as a signal it was time to leave.

"Good to see you, my friend," the older man called as Phillip headed for the door. "Don't be a stranger, stop in just to say hello once in a while. Doesn't have to be business." He opened the envelope and glanced at the contract. "You really have been very busy, I see. Congratulations on snagging this new customer, he's a well-established name in the business and you must have been quite a salesman to get him to leave his previous supplier, the one he's been with forever."

Phillip smiled his thanks, and stopped at Claudia's desk on his way out to say goodbye and added he hoped he'd run into her in town one of these days. Little did he know that someday she'd tease him about the way he often used those last four words. But on this day he meant them, and hoped it would be soon.

He spotted her one Saturday a few weeks later, looking at the window display in a small new boutique called Cristina's. He approached her from behind and tapped her shoulder lightly. She jumped, startled, and then laughed when she recognized him.

"Sorry," he said, smiling, "but remember, I told you I hoped I'd run into you. Didn't mean to scare you, though."

They exchanged small talk for a few minutes, commenting on the new shops appearing in downtown Pine Ridge and how great it was to have good weather on the weekend for a change. He was pleased to discover that outside of the office she was warm and friendly, and he was especially intrigued by her eyes, which seemed to change color with the shifting light. Glancing at his watch, he saw it was a little past noon and asked if she'd like to have lunch with him at the Purple Cow. Her response was immediate.

"Yes! I was busy daydreaming and didn't realize it was time for lunch. I'm starving all of a sudden, now that you mentioned the Cow. I love their mushroom and Swiss burger, and their fries are out of this world."

"A girl after my own heart. Let's go!"

Phillip had been very cautious about becoming involved with another woman, still nursing the wound Amanda had inflicted six years before. It had never really healed. The stitches had not gotten strong enough to hold his heart together whenever he heard their song on the car radio or when he happened to be making calls in East Lansing. He would find himself unable to resist the urge to drive past the house he had lived in, the house where they'd spent that last night. Everything there brought her back, and he realized, finally, that he had to get hold of himself, do whatever business he needed to do and get the hell out of there, the faster the better.

Dating proved somewhat therapeutic. He enjoyed having cocktails and dinner and going to movies and plays with attractive women, dates that often culminated in satisfying sex and a good night's sleep. Surely it beat getting out of a bed with sheets twisted from restlessness to look at a clock that told him dawn was still hours away. Those were the nights when the unanswered question would not stop reverberating in his brain as he paced through the small apartment. How could she have betrayed his trust? He'd believed her with every fiber of his being when she swore he was her true love, her soul mate, that there could never be anyone else for her. Believed in the plan they meticulously crafted together on that long-ago windy March night, the plan she so carelessly shredded and tossed into the ashcan of lost dreams. Certain he could never risk going through that hell again, he shielded his heart from any relationship that bore even a hint of turning into anything other than casual affection and mutual enjoyment. Until Claudia.

From the start he pinpointed the chance lunch at the Purple Cow as the day and time something told him this girl was going to figure prominently in his life. He was thirty-one and she was just two years younger, which surprised him because he had guessed her to be in her early twenties. There was a freshness about her, a kind of little-girl quality he found charming and endearing. They had dawdled over that lunch, neither seeming to want to end it, so it seemed natural to suggest walking through the park to take advantage of the nice weather.

"I love this time of year, early spring," she said, pointing to a maple. Look at the buds on this tree. The leaves are ready to pop out, and right now they look like miniature bouquets, don't they?"

He followed her gaze. "They do. You're absolutely right. My favorite month, though, is May, when the leaves first come out and they're that shade of green…"

"I know what you mean, that very tender young color before they get darker as summer progresses." Her eyes sparkled with excitement. "And of course there's nothing like the blossoms on the fruit trees, all pink and white."

"Pretty special, I agree. At home the cherry and apple trees were spectacular when they bloomed. My Mom used to call it paradise."

"Really? That was the word my Mom used when the lilacs were in bloom. They took over almost our whole back yard, and when you went out there or even opened a window, it would hit you like a wave of the best perfume you ever smelled. There's no other scent like it. Our house would be full of bouquets everywhere, and all the years I was in elementary school, I kept my teachers supplied with them. I'd carry them to school in jars my Mom had this thing about saving. She must have had a hundred of them stashed in a cupboard in the garage."

"And of course taking those lilacs to your teachers couldn't have hurt your chances of making you the perennial star pupil," he said teasingly.

"Maybe." She looked thoughtful. "I actually was a teacher's pet, and that didn't always make me the most popular kid in my class."

They parted reluctantly, but not before he asked her for her phone number and she opened her purse and wrote it on a piece of note paper. He kept glancing at it all the way home, and realized he was smiling.

She was special. He knew in some deep part of himself that she was not going to be someone he would wine and dine and end up in bed with for casual sex. No, he was going to go slowly with her, letting her take the lead as far as intimacy was concerned. But to his growing delight and excitement, he found her increasingly more responsive each time they embraced and kissed after a dinner date or a movie followed by a nightcap at a quiet local bar where the lights were low and the music romantic. At those times it was he who kept things from spinning out of control, he who gently and with great reluctance disengaged her arms and walked her to the door amid her soft protests. He wanted her desperately but not like this, not like a couple of horny teenagers in a car in front of her house. It would be in a setting worthy of the woman he already knew would be his wife.

They had discovered a new restaurant called Jamie's on the Lake, and it quickly became their favorite place for dinner. The owner began taking a special interest in the attractive young couple, and on Saturday nights he saved a table for them, a private one at a window overlooking the water. Often they were presented with complimentary glasses of champagne.

It was in the middle of an excellent fresh-caught perch dinner on the last Saturday night in May that she almost casually proposed spending the night together. He was stunned. True to his resolve to let her initiate intimacy, more than once he had fought the temptation to suggest winding up the evening at his place after their dates. She had been there once, early in their relationship, too soon for him to suggest anything more than an after-dinner drink, and after that he'd held off because he was unsure of her response. Now she had done it, struck the match with a boldness that set him on fire.

Before he could respond, she said "We've waited long enough, haven't we? Your apartment is perfect, Phillip. You pick the time, and I'll arrange to be gone for the night. I'll come up with something, maybe a grown-up girls' pajama party. What do you think about a week from tonight?"

He found his voice. "What do I think? My God, Claudia, what is there to think about? You just sent me over the moon! Of course, anything you say, any time you say." He almost knocked the wine glass over reaching for her hand.

The week crawled past so slowly it bordered on excruciating. He was finding it difficult to concentrate when he made his calls, rare for a man who usually relished contacting people with whom he'd developed friendships while doing business. He wrapped up the week on Friday afternoon in Traverse City after taking his oldest customer to lunch, and was heading for his car when he passed a small store with a sign that read "Fine Imported Linens". He stopped, turning back for a closer look. His eye had been caught by the window display which featured a miniature bed made up in a set of blue linens edged with lace, and he was hit by a sudden thought. The bed. The one element he hadn't considered when he'd spent so much time meticulously selecting the perfect candleholders, the best wine, and of course the album with the most romantic background music. Striking his forehead with his hand, he said aloud "Idiot! Why didn't I think of it? Was I really going to use those ratty old worn sheets I took from my Mom's Goodwill pile?"

He opened the door and was greeted by an attractive elderly woman. He was the lone customer, and she gave him her full attention, sensing that this handsome young man surely had a very special rendezvous in mind when he told her he was interested in the linens on the little bed in the window.

"Oh, that set. Yes, it is lovely, that color. I think it is called robin's egg blue." She spoke with an accent that complemented her regal bearing. "But I regret to tell you I sold the last set yesterday. However, you may be interested in some new linens that arrived just last week. There are some beautiful floral patterns, for instance."

"Yes, I would like to look at some. Something, maybe, that looks like spring flowers?" He was remembering the day they had lunch and walked in the park afterward.

Magda Kilczer was an astute business woman, but also a romantic Hungarian American. Yes, this young man was anticipating a tryst with a woman and she had the perfect solution for his quest.

"Give me one moment," she said after a thoughtful pause, and disappeared around a corner at the back of the store. Minutes later, she returned with a package that she held up before his incredulous eyes. A set of bed linens, sprigs of lavender lilacs and tiny green leaves strewn in an artfully fashioned random pattern on a field of pure white.

"These just arrived. I think this may be your lucky day. You will not find such beautiful adornment for the bed in a department store," she said in her elegant accent, "only in a boutique like mine. It comes from France and I must tell you it is very expensive."

"I'm sure it is, and whatever the price, I will pay it gladly because it is perfect."

She smiled. "What a lovely young man you are, so romantic. For that, I will give you a discount. Ten percent."

He started to object, but she hushed him with a flick of her long fingers, one of which bore a diamond-studded band with a sapphire in the center. She disappeared again and came back with the beautifully wrapped package, presenting it with a flourish. He handed her the check and she passed the parcel to him over the counter. Even with the generous discount it was very expensive, yet he gladly would have written a check for twice the amount without batting an eyelash. Whistling, he clutched his treasure closely as he walked to his car to begin the drive toward home, toward tomorrow night with Claudia.

It was a perfect evening for opening all the windows in the apartment, letting in the balmy early June breeze. He watched the thin white curtains billowing in the living room, and then he walked into the bedroom. Which side of the bed would she choose? The one nearest the window, probably. He walked over to smooth the pillow case, smiling as he visualized her shiny dark hair spread on it. The feel of the silky softness beneath his fingers told him it had been certainly more than worth the price. Finally satisfied with the way everything looked, he left to pick her up.

"You look beautiful," he said, opening the door and putting her small overnight bag on the back seat, "and I see you've packed some things for your pajama party with the girls. After I take you to dinner, of course, and drop you off."

She giggled. "Oh, yes, and I know the girls will just flip over the little number I picked up at Cristina's a couple of days ago. But this is the funniest part…are you ready?" Not waiting for his response, she said "They know what's going on, Uncle Gerry and Aunt Margaret, but they have to pretend they don't. I'm sure they haven't forgotten what it was like when they were young. Right now they're probably laughing their heads off. Pajama party indeed! I love those two, and I really love the way they treat me, like the daughter they never had."

"They're lucky to have you, even though…"

"Yes, I know, you mean the way it came about, suddenly losing not one but both my parents. It was so devastating, I didn't think I would ever get through the pain. My parents! Watching them leave the house, telling them how great they looked because they did. I loved the dress my Mom had found in her favorite store. Her favorite color too, sky blue. She was so excited, and I knew they were going to have a wonderful time at the party with their best friends. And then never seeing them alive again!" Her eyes had filled with tears and she let them run down her cheeks. It took a few moments before she was able to speak again.

"But I had a good job, and forcing myself to get up and go to work every day was the therapy I needed. That, and a bunch of very good friends. It took a long time for me to make myself sell the house, though, and who knows, I might still be there if Uncle Gerry hadn't convinced me that they really needed me. That got me going, and it was the beginning of the journey that led to my being here with you right now."

They had just pulled into Jamie's, and she added "Life is so strange, isn't it? There's no way of knowing what lies ahead, the worst things but sometimes the best, too. I'm sure I'll never be able to forget the feeling of having my world fall apart, and I'll never stop missing my parents as long as I live. But they're gone, and nothing can bring them back. Yet somehow it has worked out that because I left Dearborn and moved here, I've found the love of my life."

He cut the engine and turned to look at her. "You know, one of the many things I love about you is your positive attitude. I can't begin to imagine what you've been through, Claudia. And it's beyond me to make sense of it, to figure out how a tragedy like that could play a role in bringing us together. Yet all I can do is thank God that however it happened, you're with me right here, right now."

"And I'm thankful too. This is hardly the place let alone the time, for getting all heavy and religious on you, Phillip, but I have to believe that old wisdom about God moving in mysterious ways. Oh boy, listen to me. I'll blame it on Uncle Gerry and Aunt Margaret encouraging me to go to that church of theirs. More than once I've walked out thinking about something their minister said, words that stuck and helped me get through those bad moments when I would really miss my parents."

They were walking up the path to the restaurant, and he put his arm around her, drawing her close and kissing the top of her head.

"I'm glad about that, Sweetheart. But enough of the past for tonight. We have the whole glorious night and all day tomorrow ahead of us, starting with a great dinner right now. Want to bet Jamie will make sure we have champagne as soon as we sit down?"

They were married four months later in the small church Gerry Chamberlin attended every Sunday. On the good days when Margaret was able to make it, Claudia joined them, and on the bad days she stayed home with her. As she'd told Phillip, the minister's thought-provoking sermons often left her feeling comforted and glad she had come. Meanwhile, Gerry's arthritis kept worsening along with his wife's illness, his knees succumbing to the stress of the physical effort involved in caregiving. Yet he never missed a Sunday service. He had come to rely on a sturdy cane for walking, and when he proudly escorted his niece to the altar on this special day, it was gaily decorated with a big white satin bow.

After the ceremony the small party gathered for a celebration on the deck at Jamie's. The weather was pure perfection, the autumn air as scintillating as the fine champagne Jamie had ready at the table, insisting it was his pleasure to provide it as a wedding gift. Overhead, not a cloud was visible in the deep cobalt blue of the October sky, swept clear now of the last remnants of summer's heat and humidity. The crystalline lake reflected trees in their full glory, fiery reds, bright yellows, and all the shades in between, mingling with the deep greens of pine and cedar and balsam and fir. Besides Phillip's parents and Claudia's aunt and uncle, the minister and both witnesses were present. Phillip had hoped to have his brother as best man, but since Gordon and Randolph had gone to Greece for an extended stay and would not return to Chicago until Thanksgiving, Bob Appleby had graciously accepted that role, giving Phillip a wink that said see, playing Cupid paid off, didn't it?

    Cristina was her maid of honor. The two young women had become good friends, and it was Cristina who found the bridal gown while in New York on a buying trip. She'd gotten it for a song, she said, through her connections. White silk with a delicate lace bodice sprinkled with tiny pearls, it was elegant in its simplicity, and perfect for Claudia in every way. She made a breathtaking picture as she walked slowly toward him, matching the halting steps of her uncle. Awaiting her at the altar, Phillip would have sworn he was gazing at an angel.

He felt Maddie's fingers gently tugging at his arm at the same time the pilot began his instructions to prepare for landing at LAX. He realized he must have fallen asleep after an excellent lunch and a glass of chardonnay.

    "I missed a lot of scenery, I guess." He grinned, clasping his seatbelt.

    "You did, but then there's always the flight back."

22

There they were, the ubiquitous southern California swimming pools, looming ever closer as the 757 began its approach into LAX. Phillip remembered his initial reaction years ago when he and Claudia arrived to begin their first midwinter vacation here. She had the window seat and he'd leaned across her to look down when she exclaimed "Phillip, you must see this!" And both had marveled at the sight of all those pools glittering in the afternoon sun like turquoise gems.

They walked out of the terminal into the sunny afternoon, and Phillip reached into his pocket for his sunglasses while Maddie scanned the lineup of vehicles.

"There she is, my darling daughter!" Maddie walked swiftly toward a cream-colored SUV, and Phillip followed with both small pieces of luggage. She had told him about Melissa as they ate lunch.

"She's the light of my life, my Melissa, and the best part of a marriage that unfortunately didn't follow the happily ever after script."

"Not all of them do, Maddie. We were blessed, those of us who did have the happily ever after."

"I'm glad for you and Claudia. My parents had that, too, most of the time anyway. The usual ups and downs, of course, raising me and a couple of rambunctious boys. Your garden variety all-American kids who gave them a fair share of grief when we went through those awful stages of knowing it all, rebelling…"

"In other words, normal, healthy, bright children."

"That's a very nice observation, Phillip. Thank you. You would have made a great father."

"Thank you. I'll never know, of course, which makes it easy to speculate about other people's children. But what about you, Maddie? How long have you been a single mother?"

"Let's see…Melissa was ten when we were divorced, so it's been about eleven years. Derek remarried a year later and moved to Montana to take over his elderly father-in-law's ranch. That was something he always dreamed of, running a ranch. They have two boys, and Melissa has told me a lot about her half-brothers. It took a while, but she's grown very fond of them and enjoys spending time up there. She likes her stepmother, she's younger than I am and seems very fond of Melissa. Derek has been very generous with child support, and he's seen to it that his only daughter always had everything she needed, and most of what she wanted. And he's never stopped. She should be spoiled but she isn't, thank God." She paused, then added "He's a good guy, really. But as it turned out he wasn't the right good guy for me. Trust me, though, I haven't given up. I'll be ready for that one when he comes along."

Long bright blonde hair streaming in the warm breeze, Melissa sprang from the SUV and dashed to hug her mother. Tossing both bags into the back of the vehicle, she motioned for Phillip to get in and opened the passenger door for Maddie, then slid into the driver's seat for a fast takeoff. It was all done with lightning speed under the glare of the approaching attendant.

"Nice," said Maddie, "done like a pro, wouldn't you say, Phillip?"

"Absolutely. And by the way, Melissa, your mother has told me a lot about you and I'm very happy to meet you."

"Oh, I feel the same way, Mr. Ashcroft. Mom told me about my Granny and you way back when you were in college together, and I think it's kind of romantic, you know?"

"I'd like you to call me Phillip. It was a long time ago, yes, and it was romantic. I look forward to seeing her again."

Granny? How could that name possibly apply to Amanda? Well, if all went according to the plan Maddie had laid out, he would find out later this afternoon. Maddie had told him during the flight that he would occupy the guest room in their condo, and that after lunch she would take him to see Amanda.

Melissa produced chilled Dungeness crab and avocado salads along with crusty sourdough rolls. Maddie filled the wine glasses with a chardonnay so delectable he sipped it very slowly, making it last, letting it linger on his tongue. Noticing his attention to the label, Maddie told him it was from a small family-owned winery that did not ship out of state, and promised she would see that he took a few bottles with him when he flew back home.

23

It was not a particularly large house, light tan stucco in the favored Spanish style with its red tiled roof and balconies on the upper floor with curved black wrought iron railings. The yard was neatly groomed, with flowering bushes surrounding the front of the house.

"So this is the house you grew up in, Maddie? It's lovely, and look at that marvelous view!"

The car had just pulled into the driveway and Maddie followed his gaze, smiling. "Thank you. And of course you know you're looking at the Santa Monica Mountains in the distance. I used to love sitting on the window seat in the living room and watching the sun disappear behind them." Glancing at the clock on the dashboard, she added "It'll be sunset in just a few hours. Meanwhile, Phillip, here we are. Are you ready?" He nodded and got out of the car.

What would she look like after all these years? And what would he look like to her? He tried to shake off the sudden attack of nerves as they approached the front door, his mind full of jumbled thoughts. What do you say to this person who once upon a time filled your entire universe? This person you never imagined you would ever see again?

He need not have worried. The door opened and there she was, Amanda, speaking easily as she looked directly at him after acknowledging her daughter with a smile. Had she, he couldn't help wondering, rehearsed her lines?

"Phillip," she said, "Welcome to my home. You really haven't changed, I see. Handsome as ever." The voice was the same as the one he had last heard on the phone that terrible July morning in Michigan, perhaps hoarsened just a bit by age.

His voice, when he finally found it, didn't sound right to his own ears, but had the strange quality of an echo.

"Amanda. Just as beautiful as I remember." The words, at least, had rolled effortlessly off his tongue, and he felt a lessening of the tension.

She smiled then, and stepped aside to let him enter after Maddie gave him a gentle push.

He knew it would be awkward, this meeting, and they might have remained standing in the living room staring at each other for God knows how long if Maddie hadn't intervened. She motioned for Phillip to sit on the sofa facing the fireplace. Amanda remained standing and broke the silence.

"What can I get for you, Phillip? And you, Maddie," she added, finally focusing her attention on her daughter, "coffee or tea? Or maybe a drink? It's not cocktail time quite yet, but I thought perhaps…"

Now she seemed nervous, and Maddie rescued her. "Good idea, Mom. Who cares what time it is? I think a drink sounds great. Why don't we have a glass of that nice chardonnay I brought you last time I came, the one you said you liked so much? It's the same one we had at lunch, Phillip," she added, and he nodded, smiling.

They stood in front of the fireplace holding their wine glasses because Maddie thought the occasion deserved a special toast. She waited for words from Phillip or her mother, but when neither spoke, she raised her glass and said "To old friends meeting again after long years." It was simple and it was appropriate, and they touched glasses and drank.

Maddie stayed just long enough to satisfy herself that things seemed to be going as well as could be expected. After she left, Phillip and Amanda sat for a while, sipping their wine and regarding each other in a silence that was not uncomfortable. She hasn't changed all that much, he is thinking, from the girl he noticed on the lawn next door to his house in East Lansing that September day. She is thinner, as Maddie had told him, maybe a little too thin, but it had the effect of making her more beautiful than a woman in her late sixties had a right to be, her features honed, sculpted. Her hair, he thought, doesn't flow in a thick mass past her shoulders anymore, and the vibrant chestnut brown has faded, with streaks of silver now instead of gold. The porcelain skin isn't quite as flawless…how could it be? But those eyes! When he looks into them, he still sees the intense blue of the depths of Lake Michigan and somehow everything else about her is transformed, and she is once again the Amanda of his youth.

Amanda broke the silence. "We seem to be taking stock of each other, Phillip. It is so strange, you know, I look at you and I don't see a man who will turn seventy in less than two years. Yes, I remember your birthday very well, always have. By some trick of memory, I am seeing the handsome young man with a headful of reddish curls I last saw so many, many years ago in Michigan. How is that possible?"

"You must have been reading my thoughts, Amanda, because I was just looking at you and experiencing the very same phenomenon. I agree it is strange, the way the mind processes images from the past, sort of like having them spring to life from an old photo album."

She seemed to consider his response for a moment, then set her glass on the end table with a forcefulness that matched her next words.

"Enough, Phillip. Let's get on with it, the reason you're sitting here right now. I have things to tell you, things you should know, things you should have known years ago. First, let me say that when I found out Maddie tracked you down and talked you into coming here, I was horrified. But then I remembered that after we had lunch one day and my tongue was loosened by wine, I told her about us. She put two and two together, my smart daughter, and figured out that on top of grieving for my dead husband, I was carrying this guilt over what I had done to you a long, long time ago. So off she went on a mission to help her poor despondent mother, and I cannot tell you how much I hated the realization that I had caused my children, Maddie especially, so much concern. But now I can confess I'm very grateful that her determination and yes, courage brought you here. And I can't find words to describe my gratitude to you for coming all this way to hear what I have to say."

He took time to respond, pausing to glance at the portrait of Brett above the fireplace. Good-looking bastard, maybe a touch pretty boy. No wonder that older woman had gone after him, starting the affair that sent Amanda to Michigan and to him. But back to the here and now, Phillip, she's waiting for you to say something. He knew he had to choose his words carefully.

"Your daughter, as you surely know, can be very persuasive. She has a way of making you want to help her if you can, and when she told me how much it would mean to her if I'd make this trip to see you, I decided to do it. And of course I would like to help you, too, Amanda. So here I am, waiting for some guidance. You need to tell me how I can help you."

She took a long sip of wine and waited for a moment or two, gathering her thoughts.

"It's hard to know where to begin, Phillip, but I guess it would have to be the last time we saw each other. That morning at the airport." Ah, that morning; she in her smart traveling outfit, waving just before she disappeared into the plane. The image no longer brought with it the bittersweet sensation he had felt for so many years, and now he could look at it without an outward show of emotion. But her next words tested that control.

"I was so much in love with you, Phillip. Walking away from you was pure torture, everything in me wanted to turn back. I thought I would surely die if I didn't see your face every day. All during that flight, I had to keep reassuring myself that our separation was just temporary, that I had to stay strong until you came to Los Angeles so we could be together for the rest of our lives. I had to hold tight to that plan we'd made together to keep myself from falling apart."

She reached for the wine bottle and divided the remainder between their glasses before she started talking again.

"Those first weeks away from you were some of the hardest of my life. Talking to you on the phone, hearing your voice, that was my lifeline. Just knowing you were there meant everything to me…"

He needed to break his silence, and he had to make a conscious effort to stem the bitterness that threatened to manifest itself in his question. "What happened, Amanda? I'd like to know what changed."

The ticking of the antique clock on the mantle was the only sound in the room for what seemed a very long time, and he could tell by the look in her eyes that she was reaching far back in memory.

"It wasn't so much what changed, Phillip, it was a matter of who changed, and of course it was I. Stepping off that plane in Los Angeles into the arms of my parents…well, of course it felt warm and comforting, but my heart was in Michigan with you. Driving to our house, they kept asking me questions, telling me all sorts of stuff, but it was hard for me to focus so I just explained that I was tired. Which of course was true. I was wiped out, physically from lack of sleep, of course, and emotionally as well. I took a little nap before dinner that day, and when my mother woke me up, she told me about Brett. She said it was all she could do to convince him not to come to the airport with them, and not to show up at dinner that first night."

"What do you mean when you say she told you about Brett?"

"Well, he had been in constant touch with them for months. I never told you he kept trying to talk to me that spring when I was in Michigan. But I wouldn't accept his calls, and he finally gave up. That was when you and I were planning what we would do after graduation and I couldn't bear the thought of him. I kept quiet about it because I just didn't want to even speak his name aloud. But he knew I'd be coming home after graduation, so he decided to just bide his time and work on my parents in the meantime."

"But you went home at Christmas. Didn't he show up then?"

"No, he and his girlfriend were still together then. Remember my telling you about Denise, that predatory siren he threw me over for? Well, it seems the affair was starting to burn itself out. They had flown off to some Caribbean island for the holidays to try to reignite it, apparently, but it didn't work and they broke up soon after they came back. Anyway, not long after that, he started talking to my parents and must have done one hell of a sales job because they gave him my phone number. That's when he started calling me. I've told you how close our families were, so it was no surprise when Brett's mother jumped in to help plead his case about how much he loved me and how deeply he regretted his fling with the older woman. So there you have it, what I was greeted with when I came home. And it only took Brett a couple of days to show up in person and start his campaign to win me back."

"Let me ask you this, Amanda. How long were you able to resist his overtures once you got back?"

She sighed, picked up her wine glass and drained it.

"Oh, God, let me think about that. To say he was persistent would be to make the understatement of all time. I tried to keep my mind focused on us, how deeply in love I was with you. I made myself think of how much pain he put me through when he betrayed me. All that, but... I don't know, Phillip, he wore me down and I have to confess it didn't take all that long before I capitulated. He managed to convince me he had turned himself back into the Brett I fell in love with when I was a teenager, the Brett I was sure would be my soul mate for life. And finally, when he asked for my forgiveness, I gave it to him. He had me feeling so sorry for him. The poor guy was practically turning himself inside out apologizing. I know that sounds dramatic, and I guess it was. I do have to interject at this point that he was a faithful husband, never strayed once all the years we were married. It was a good marriage, a very good one. I couldn't have asked for a better husband and father for my children. That one fling before we were even engaged was it, and looking back at how young he was then and how irresistible she must have been, I can pretty much understand how it happened."

His gaze did not falter as he looked at her, thinking of that time long years ago when she had convinced him that he, Phillip, was destined to play that very role of soul mate in the future they planned together with such youthful hope and enthusiasm. So he had his answer at last. Brett had the advantage of proximity once she returned home, and apparently the power to win her back. Now he glanced again at the portrait, and sent a silent message: "Congratulations."

Amanda rose and disappeared into the kitchen. When she returned she was holding a newly-opened bottle of wine, and poured some into each glass before she spoke again.

"I need this," she explained, "for courage. There's more I have to tell you, Phillip. Take a long drink because you'll need it too."

When he complied, she said simply "I was pregnant."

Reflecting on the conversation much later, he recalled that at first he received her explanation for the suddenness of the marriage calmly and without rancor. It was the classic age-old reason in that era, and it was referred to as a shotgun wedding; when you got pregnant, you married the father as quickly as arrangements could be made. It made complete sense, and he accepted it at face value. After all, in that last dreadful phone conversation she admitted she'd been sleeping with Brett. Now, looking back from the vantage point offered by the passage of so many years, he saw how youthfully naïve he had been, behaving as if the world had come to an end when he learned that she had leaped into Brett's arms, into his bed with such speed. Could he really have remained mired in that swamp of self-pity and anger for all those years? Of course he hadn't known the whole story then. Her first love reappearing on the scene full of remorse and longing for her, she capitulating to his pleadings. Then there were her parents encouraging the match, and her desire to please them. It was all so understandable, and it was so far in the past that he found himself sitting here now with no lingering animosity. Instead, he was surprised to feel his heart expand with sympathy for the frightened and confused young woman she must have been. Remembering her sobs at the end of that final phone call, he could imagine how heavily on her conscience had lain the knowledge that she had broken his heart. If Maddie was right and he could help her by listening to her, he was glad of the opportunity. Look at how it all had worked out. She just told him she had a great marriage with Brett and what the hell, he bore her no ill will because that was exactly what he had with Claudia. In the end everyone won.

He had taken a couple of long sips as he listened to her, and now he smiled at her as he set his glass on the coffee table.

"Amanda, listen to me. Yes, it's true you broke my heart that day, and it did take a very long time before I was able to entrust it to someone else. But eventually I did, when I fell in love with Claudia. So it turned out we both had happy marriages even though we lost our mates much too soon. If you're in need of forgiveness from me, please know you have it. Now that you've told me so very clearly the predicament you were in at the time, I think I can understand, as much as a man can, what you must have gone through. But good God, you weren't the first young woman to have second thoughts about an old love reappearing in your life, nor the first to marry quickly. It wasn't like today. In those days pregnancy was a compelling reason, and Brett was man enough to do the right thing."

"It wasn't exactly like that, Phillip," she began quietly, but he interrupted, determined to make her see how completely he understood.

"However it happened, Amanda, it doesn't matter at this point. I'm glad Maddie asked me to come here. Having all this finally brought to light should free you from that old guilt and get that monkey off your back. Yes, it's true that all these years I've let it simmer on some level deep inside me, not being able to understand why you did what you did. But you just made me see the total picture. People talk a lot about closure these days, and I see this as our chance to achieve it and finally close the book shut. Would you agree?"

"No." She got up and walked across the room to the large bay window that framed the mountains. She stood there, her back to him, for what struck Phillip as a very long time before she spoke again. When she did, she turned to face him but stayed where she was.

"We can't have closure yet, because there is more to tell you, as I said." Her gaze was steady and her words came slowly, devoid of drama. "It's about the pregnancy. The child I was carrying was not Brett's, Phillip. That little girl was ours, yours and mine. Maddie is your biological daughter."

Phillip's immediate reaction was disbelief. Later he would recognize it as a reflexive way of protecting himself from shock. But now he got up from the sofa and walked over to confront her. The look on his face made her take a step back.

"Jesus Christ, Amanda, how can you say that? You told me you slept with him not long after you came back. How on earth could you possibly have decided he wasn't the father?"

"Because," she responded, trying to keep her tone calm and matter-of-fact, "I started to suspect I might be pregnant two weeks after I left you when I didn't get my period as I should have. But I told myself no, it's not supposed to be all that unusual to miss a period or have it show up late, even though that had never happened to me before. It was always like clockwork with me. Then I thought, well, I've been under a lot of stress, all the emotion surrounding those weeks before graduation, the flight home, and then having to deal with Brett's sudden entry into my life again. But after a full month passed and nothing happened, that was when I knew for sure."

"But how could that be, Amanda?" He wasn't ready to let go of his disbelief. "We never took chances. We used contraceptives every time, or rather, I did." He nodded as though agreeing with himself. He'd always acted responsibly, hadn't he?

"Yes, except for that final night and morning when that was the last thing on our minds. When we thought, or at least I did if I thought at all, was what the hell, we're going to be married soon anyway. Remember?"

Oh yes, he remembered. God, yes. Now it was all coming back. No thought of consequences on his part either that evening; the sensual impact of drinking fine champagne, the long, virtually sleepless night of desperate lovemaking, then the achingly sweet finale in the warm shower the next morning…

"What fun the fates must have had playing with us, with our lives." She had turned to look out the window again. "I keep reading and hearing about how difficult it can be for some couples to achieve pregnancy, how hard they try, what lengths they're willing to go to and how much money they're willing to spend. But you and I, throwing caution to the winds for just a few hours out of all those months of being so careful…" She shook her head.

Memories assaulted his mind, painful memories of all he and Claudia had gone through to conceive a child -- the fertility tests, the pills, the hope and subsequent disappointment, all part of a frustrating pattern that became a routine part of their lives for so long. He recalled what the young doctor told them on their final visit, her eyes sympathetic behind huge glasses with bright red frames. He still remembered her name. Stanton. Dr. Cecilia Stanton. "Hopefully something new will come along, but for now it looks as though we've pretty much exhausted all the available treatments for infertility. You can be sure I'll contact you if something new pops up, something we haven't tried. Meanwhile, try to relax and just enjoy your lives as much as you can. Sometimes there's no obvious reason for the lack of ability to conceive. Neither party may lack normal fertility, but the ovum might harbor an allergy to the sperm. I've read about it, and I've also heard it's possible it can remedy itself, but I don't have firsthand knowledge of an instance where something like that actually happened. I wish it would happen for you, you are such nice people." She rose from the chair behind her desk and offered her hand. "I am so sorry."

Allergy. Certainly there had been no allergy problem with this woman. He had to believe her because there was no reason for her to lie, and now the reality struck with a force so overwhelming he felt lightheaded, as though he might faint, something he'd never done in his whole life. He felt the blood drain out of him, and reached blindly to the wall next to the window to steady himself. He had a child! He, Phillip Ashcroft, was the father of a daughter, the woman he had come to know as Maddie Schuster.

"Phillip? Are you okay?" She looked at him with real concern. "I can see you're in a state of shock. It was clumsy of me to just announce it the way I did. I'm sorry. I should have done it differently, should have prepared you…"

No question, his emotions were on a rollercoaster ride. In truth, he didn't know what he was feeling right now. The disbelief was gone, replaced by a mixture of anger, sorrow and wonder, and he had to take a few minutes to sort it all out before he could respond.

Anger won. His flushed face betrayed him even before he spoke, a tremor in his voice as he started talking, then strengthening and rising to a level that made her take a step backwards.

"Shock, you say? Just how the bloody hell is a guy supposed to react to this kind of news? What difference does it make how you dropped this bomb, Amanda? The fact is, you did it. Look at you, standing right in front of me and calmly breaking the news that you had my child short of a half century ago but never allowed me to know about her. That's so unfair, so unjust -- no, worse than that, it's sinful, pure evil. For God's sake, woman, how could you not have the decency to tell me you were pregnant, that I was the father of the baby you were carrying? What sort of human being are you?"

He could see the effort she was making to swallow her tears before she spoke. "Okay, I deserved that. But the question ought to be what sort of human being was I then, and I'll tell you the answer. I was a very scared one, Phillip, terrified, if you want to know the truth. Yes, I know," waving her hand, "you can't bring yourself to link me with the word truth, and God knows I can't blame you. I lied to you back then, but everything I've told you today is absolutely true, including what I'm about to say. And if you take it as a preposterous excuse, trying to justify what I did, well, I'll have to accept that."

"Go ahead, please. If nothing else, it should be interesting." The flare of anger was subsiding. "I've got to sit down, though, and try to calm   myself. I could really use something stronger but I guess I'll have to make do with wine."

"I have whiskey and brandy, both kind of old…" He stopped her, shaking his head, and made his way back to the sofa. She followed and refilled their glasses before she sat and started talking.

"Nobody who hasn't been there can possibly imagine how I felt. Not all that long out of my teens, pregnant and panicked. And right there at my side was Brett, begging me to marry him. He'd been hired by the agency where he worked as an intern, got the job without the help of his lover as it turned out, and kept moving up the so-called ladder there. According to my parents, he was known in their social circle as a go-getter and a rising star."

"That was it?" He interrupted sharply. "He had this great career going for him and that was why you decided to marry him? You didn't think I could get a job out here that would let me provide for you and the baby? I should say, our baby?"

"I wasn't thinking that way then, Phillip. Okay, I promised truth, and yes, that was part of it, his doing so well and offering security, my parents so obviously approving…you and I, well, we were kids just barely out of college, and he had a whole year on us. But I'm not a whore, Phillip. It wasn't like I sold myself to the higher bidder. I did fall back in love with him, and it did happen quickly. It's impossible to explain how I felt. It was as though I'd gotten on a train that was going so fast all I wanted to do was sit back without really thinking about anything except what was happening to me and what to do about it. It seemed like the best solution at the time."

This time it was he who got up and crossed the room to look out the window. The sunset was spectacular, and he remembered Maddie talking about this being her favorite spot. Now he understood, watching the red orb that seemed to teeter atop the slightly rounded tip of a mountain. Maddie. His daughter. He was still trying to absorb this amazing new discovery.

"I'm trying, really trying," he said, not turning to look at her, "but I can't seem to shake this god-awful thing you've hit me with, Amanda. It's like I'm being smothered by a…a heavy cloak and I can't fight my way out from under it. I don't think you have any idea of what you've done to me this afternoon. You've told a man who always longed for a child of his own that he had one all that time and never knew she existed. Never got to look at her newborn face. Never got to see her take her first steps, hear her first words. Never got to see her graduate from high school or college. Or walk her down the aisle when she got married. I never got to know she gave birth to my grandchild. My God, Amanda. Do you have any idea, can you even begin to imagine how suddenly finding out about all those losses makes me feel?"

"I think I can." She had walked over to him and stood beside him, making him turn to look at her. "I know I did a horrible thing, Phillip, and maybe I never should have told you. It might have been better to let sleeping dogs lie."

"Just out of curiosity, why did you choose to tell me now?"

"Selfishness, I guess." Her response was unhesitating. "It's a way of getting rid of the guilt I've carried all these years. Which is why it turns out I'm fine with Maddie finding you and getting you to come here, after all. Brett is dead and I still have that to deal with, but as Maddie pointed out to me, confessing what I did to you is at least going to lighten the load a little. Hopefully."

He was struck by a sudden thought. "You didn't so much as hint, did you, about my being her…"

"God, no!" She interrupted him, shouting, a horrified expression on her face. "No, she still grieves for her father and I couldn't do that to her. Brett was the only father she'd ever known, and he truly was the best. He cherished his only daughter and loved her from the moment she came into the world."

"Why wouldn't he? She was his firstborn, after all. Surely he believed he was her biological father, right?"

"No, you're not right. As much of a liar as you believe me to be, that time I did tell the truth. To be totally honest, I didn't want to at first. In fact, I was the aggressor when it came to sex, thinking I could get away with it, that he would have no reason not to believe he'd gotten me pregnant. The timing I figured I could deal with later. But something happened to me when I realized the wedding date had been set and was fast approaching. I was going to marry him, and unless I told the truth, the marriage was going to be built on a lie. I had to tell him I was pregnant with your child. If that meant he didn't want to marry me, then I'd have to figure out my next move. As I said, I wasn't exactly thinking straight at the time. But you know, Phillip, telling him the truth did not change his mind, not in the least. He said nobody else needed to know, and he would love that child as though he were indeed the biological father. He said that after all, the woman he loved was carrying that baby, and he went so far as to tell me I had every right to fall into another man's arms and bed after what he did to me. Those words took away any doubt that I was doing the best thing. They made me really, really fall deeply in love with him. I can't expect you to understand how a woman can be in love with two men at the same time, but I swear to God that is exactly what happened to me back then. You were still in my heart. I hadn't stopped loving you. I never forgot you and I never forgot what we once had together. And on some level I still love you, impossible as that is for you to believe."

He listened closely to her long, impassioned speech. No, he thought, I never will understand any of this, but so be it. Can any man honestly claim to really understand women? Sighing, he turned away from her, not trusting himself to look into those beautiful deep blue eyes while he spoke.

"It isn't impossible for me to believe what you're saying, Amanda. That's different than understanding it, which I admit is difficult. But I believe you for this reason: I never could let go of you completely, try as I might. I believe it would be hard to find anyone whose first real love does not reside exclusively and forever in some small place in his or her heart, and I am no exception. I loved Claudia as much as any man can love a woman, but you were always locked in a secret place deep inside me. And even now, even though I'm very close to hating you – yes, hating you – for what you've done, I know you'll always stay there."

She moved closer to him and they stood quietly, watching the changing hues in the sky above the mountains where the sun had lingered before slipping completely from view.

"Sometimes," she said after a long silence, "I think about that last day in East Lansing, and the black-haired woman who sold me the crystal glasses for the champagne you bought. I still remember the wistful look in her eyes when she started to give me the package, then decided to tie a fancy ribbon around the box before she handed it to me again. That ribbon was her gift, her way of wishing me happiness, at least that's what I wanted to believe then, and I always will."

"And I think you're absolutely right. It's one of those things we all experience in life. We do something, say something that can unintentionally trigger an emotion in another person. A memory, good or bad, or perhaps regret for a chance that was missed. Who knows?" He paused and turned to look at her before he spoke again.

"This is what I remember, Amanda. Standing in the kitchen of my house, looking at the sun setting, just as we're doing right now. No mountains, just an ordinary Michigan sunset, but beautiful beyond words. Because we were young and in love. Because of the way it lit up those gold streaks in your hair. Some images remain permanently imprinted on our memory, and that is certainly one of them."

She put her hand on his arm. "It was no ordinary Michigan sunset, Phillip. It was extraordinary. But there's something else I must tell you. When Maddie called to tell me what she had done, that you were coming here, I found myself imagining being with you again, how I would feel. Now I know. But she also told me about Karla, so you're safe. For now," she added, laughing, "but I can't guarantee it indefinitely, so I'd better call Maddie. She has a special place in mind for us to have dinner."

They were sitting in the living room waiting for Maddie and Melissa when Amanda said there was a question she needed to ask.

"As I told you, Phillip, Maddie has no idea that Brett is not her biological father. I was tempted to tell her many times after that lunch when I gave in to her pleadings to open up and let her know one of the reasons I had gone into my shell. I told her about our college romance, and after I found out she had tracked you down and succeeded in having you agree to come here, I was even more sorely tempted to tell her the truth. But I didn't, even though her father's death had removed any question of how her knowing might affect their relationship. As I said, she was grieving too, and I just couldn't even think of it. Can you understand that?" He nodded and started to speak, but she held up her hand to stop him.

"Good. Now that you know the whole story, you have every right to tell her it is your DNA that comprises half of her gene pool. So here's my question: do you think you might want to do that some day? I must tell you it would be perfectly okay with me."

It took a long time before he could formulate a response. There was far too much to absorb to consider the possibility she had just broached. But she was waiting, and he tried to answer as honestly as possible.

"I don't know, Amanda. Probably not. Telling her would be almost certain to shake the very foundation of her life, and what would it accomplish? Would it be worth the risk?"

She started to speak but here was Maddie at the front door, and Melissa sitting in the SUV in the driveway, waiting.

They sat, the four of them, at a table in a restaurant on the end of a pier in Malibu. The Pacific was made barely visible by the last lingering rays of sunset, casting just enough light to see the surf as it approached before disappearing beneath them. Amanda looked at the menu for just a moment, then laid it aside and watched Phillip studying the younger women as they pored over theirs. There was a hunger in his gaze, as though he could not get enough of searching their faces for visual clues relating to his newfound knowledge. Yes, he was thinking, there it is, the most obvious one. Maddie's eyes. He suddenly recalled the way they had struck him the first time they met, the night she came to his home. Amber, green-rimmed, tilted slightly upwards at the outer corners. His mother's eyes, of course, swimming in that gene pool, finding their way to the granddaughter she would never know she had.

It was full dark when they finished eating, and Phillip took one last look at the ocean, the gentle swells now glistening under the restaurant's spotlights, before following the women out onto the pier. When he climbed into the vehicle, he settled back with a yawn he tried to suppress but couldn't, entirely. He was aware that Amanda had noticed, watching him. When they reached her house, he shook off the weariness that had seeped into his bones, and escorted her to the door while the younger women waited in the car. She turned the key in the lock, then turned to him, smiling.

"I could tell the girls to go on, you know, and ask you in for a nightcap and drive you to Maddie's later. But I won't, Phillip, because you must be exhausted. You had to have gotten up very early this morning to fly across the country, and this day surely has been long and draining for both of us, hasn't it?"

"Yes, it has, and yes, I am exhausted. My brain is so full of everything I've learned, it feels close to either bursting or closing down from lack of sleep. I'll choose the latter and head for the bed Maddie has waiting for me as quickly as good manners will permit."

"Oh, she'll understand. Young though she is, she has to be very tired too. I know I am. I feel as if my emotions have been whirled in the spin cycle of a modern washer and then put through the wringer of an old-fashioned one."

"Good analogy, couldn't describe what I've been feeling all day any better. Will we see each other tomorrow?" He waited for her answer with mixed emotions. She shook her head slowly.

"I think it would be better if we make this our last encounter, Phillip. I feel we've said all there is to say, and prolonging it could prove painful. You know? We've stirred up enough old memories, maybe more than enough, and it's time to put the past to rest once and for all. You've been wonderful, coming all this way to help me, and really, I can't thank you enough."

It was the answer he was hoping for. "You're more than welcome, and you're right. It's best to end it like this, now that everything is finally out in the open. Naturally, it'll take time for me to sort it all out, but I'll never regret making this trip. And to think I made at it the request of my daughter!"

He paused for a moment and glanced up at the sky before meeting her eyes, those incredible eyes shining clear in the starlight, for what he knew would be the final time. His voice turned husky with the last words he would ever say to this woman.

"Before we say good-bye, I want you to know I'm very happy to hear you say I helped you by coming here. Hopefully, you can finally shed that burden you've been carrying all these years."

"I'll try, Phillip. It has been there for such a long time, but yes, now I can let it go and focus on all the positive things in my life."

He gripped her shoulders and looked at her with a new intensity.

"But know this, Amanda, and never forget it. What you did for me today by telling me something you did not have to, something I never would have suspected in a million years, has brought an entirely new dimension to my life. You know you could have told me about how much pressure you were under to reunite with Brett, and let it go at that. You could have chosen to keep secret forever the fact that you were pregnant with my child, and nobody ever would have known about it. But you didn't, and when you told me Maddie is my daughter, you made me realize that a door I always thought had been shut to me, actually did open once, if only for a fleeting moment in time. And this is your true gift to me: As long as I live, I will always know I am a father, after all."

One last kiss of fond farewell between two people who long ago loved each other passionately, and then he walked to the waiting vehicle. She remained standing at the door, watching until the tail lights were no longer visible.

24

She was a magnet, hair shining gold in the brightly lit terminal as he stepped off the tram. He would have sworn he could feel his heart leave his body as he headed straight for her. She had started toward him but stopped short, searching his face. Phillip closed the remaining distance at a slow run, then set down his small bag and the package Maddie had rightly assured him would make it through security at LAX. No words were exchanged as he wrapped her in an embrace that took the breath out of her.

"I missed you!" She managed to say it between kisses. "I'm so happy you're back! I thought you might stay longer."

"I couldn't stand the thought of another day without you."

"We have to get out of here. People are looking at us. What's in the package?"

"Hell with them, they're probably jealous. Oh, you gorgeous creature, you're right, we have to get out of here. So I can kiss you properly."

"If that didn't qualify as properly just now, I say let's get going. But the package, what's in it?"

"Nothing much, just the best chardonnay you've ever tasted, and wait till you hear who gave it to me at the airport."

"Let me take a wild guess. Had to be that charming redhead, your old flame's daughter."

"Yes, you're right, but there's so much more to tell you. You'll have to wait, though, till I get this travel grime showered off me, and we're relaxing over cocktails before I give you a full report"

"You're going to make me wait that long? You're mean!"

"Consider it a chance to hone your patience skills."

"You're teasing me, you know, but okay, I can wait. What about dinner, though? You must be starving."

"Come to think of it, I am. Want to stop at the crab place? We'll be going right past it."

"Nope. Again, I have to turn down your nice invitation. I guess we'll just have to make a special trip there some day for a great crab dinner, but not tonight No stops till Banyan Bay, where a wonderful bouillabaisse I slaved over all morning sits in my fridge waiting to be heated up and eaten with some nice warm crusty French bread. Oh, and accompanied by that special wine you bragged about!"

"Sounds fabulous. Why is the speed limit on this interstate so damned low?"

"Okay, let's have it, you with the mysterious look in your eye." They were having cocktails and appetizers on the balcony, wearing sweaters against the chill. "I don't need to hear every detail, just tell me if going there with Maddie accomplished what she hoped it would. When you left, did you think your visit helped?"

He took a long sip of the Manhattan. "If I can take to heart what Amanda said to me at the end of that long, long day, then I'd have to conclude it did help. I listened to her very emotional account of what took place some forty-five years ago because Maddie asked me to. I went there thinking okay, I'll hear her out if that's what it takes, but it happened such a long time ago, it doesn't make any difference now. I'm not going to pass judgment, just listen. But you know what, Karla? She did make me understand the whole thing. She actually made me see the young, pregnant, frightened girl she was then and why she made the decisions she did with all that was happening in her world."

She waited for a few minutes before she spoke, nodding. "And just as you implied, it is now ancient history. Sounds like things worked out for both of you, you with your happy marriage, Amanda with hers even though that one began with the classic shotgun wedding. Back then, the father-to-be married his pregnant bride. Just like Caleb and yours truly."

He set his drink on the broad arm of the deck chair. "Not exactly like you and Caleb. You were carrying Caleb's baby, you see, and he's the man you married. Amanda was carrying mine. That was the difference."

He said it in a conversational tone. In fact, the statement sounded almost matter-of-fact, and perhaps the delayed impact was what caused her to react the way she did. She stared at him open-mouthed, and let go of the glass that was halfway to her lips. Then she simply sat, unmoving and looking at the fragments of broken crystal and the spreading pool of its contents before she found her voice.

"My God, Phillip, I've heard of news that makes your jaw drop, but you just made my hand drop a good crystal cocktail glass!"

The fire lent an air of coziness as they ate the aromatic bouillabaisse and drank the chilled chardonnay. He'd insisted on making her another martini, having accurately surmised she needed it. When he handed it to her, she sipped and set it down ever so carefully, then watched him take charge of removing the fragments and wiping the tiled balcony floor.

By the time they were inside eating dinner, he'd reported most of the events of the past three days. Maddie had persuaded him to stay longer so that he could visit the places she called "My L.A." and dine at her favorite spots. One was a sushi restaurant in Malibu, and he chuckled as he told Karla the way Melissa related her hilarious description of a lunch there with Amanda.

"Remember the first time I talked Granny into taking me here for lunch, Mom?" The question was addressed to Maddie, but she turned to Phillip, explaining. "Mom knows the story. I think I was about thirteen. Anyway, I thought her eyes would pop right out of her head when she saw the sashimi I ordered. Well, she said, I'm certainly not going to eat raw fish, and when she saw me dig into it, I could tell she was preparing to take me to the emergency room. She had taken a little bite out of a California roll only because I lied and told her the tiny chunk of tuna was cooked but still had that red color. Oh, and the salad. She slid hers over to me and said, if eating seaweed is your idea of fine dining, sweetie, here, have mine too. But just a couple of weeks ago she called me to have lunch with her, and guess where she suggested we meet? Yep, right here, and even though she still wasn't quite brave enough to go for the sashimi, she ate what she called seaweed along with the miso soup and sushi, and I'd have to say she ate it all with gusto."

"I love your granddaughter sight unseen." Karla was laughing too. "I still can't believe I'm hearing you, or myself for that matter, say that word. Granddaughter."

"I know." He shook his head and stared into the fire. "Somehow this whole episode seems to have the quality of a dream. I have trouble believing I actually have a daughter and a granddaughter."

"Speaking of the former, do you think Maddie will come back here, now she's accomplished what she set out to do?"

"Oh yes, at least for the month or so remaining on her lease. And who knows, she may come back again from time to time. She did say she really enjoys being here on the Gulf Coast. I may have told you what she does for a living. She writes for trade magazines, technical stuff mostly, but what she enjoys most is the occasional chance to interview and do personal profiles on various people in the auto-related industries. In today's world, one can work from almost anywhere using computers and cell phones and such. I recognized at least one of those publications from my working days. She told me the atmosphere here helps her creative juices flow. She likes walking where it's so quiet she can listen to birdsong and the rustle of leaves on the palm trees, she said. Unlike the hustle and bustle that is Los Angeles. And she absolutely loves our powdered-sugar beaches."

"Wouldn't it be great if she decided to come back regularly? What a wonderful thing that would be, Phillip, to see more of your daughter."

"It would be pure heaven. When I said goodbye to her and Melissa at the airport, they both kissed me and kept thanking me, and Maddie said she could feel a strong connection with me. That floored me. If only she knew! I confess I didn't board that plane exactly dry-eyed."

He had poured the rest of the wine and Karla waited a moment, sipping slowly before she spoke.

"I know this is still very new to you, and maybe it's much too soon to even bring this up, but I am curious. So I have to ask you if you think you'll tell her at some point about being her biological father. I mean, you did say Amanda gave you the green light if you ever feel like doing it."

"True. She asked me if I thought I would and I guess I'll give you the same answer. I really don't know right now, but I think probably I won't. As I told her, there is a strong probability it would shake the very foundation of her life, and I don't think it's a risk worth taking."

"It's very hard for me to process all this, Philip, and it has to be even more so for you still. I mean, just like that, out of the blue, you have a family. A real biological family. A daughter and a granddaughter."

He nodded. "Yes, I know. I longed for a family of our own all those years, but once every possible effort to conceive a child failed, I tried to downplay that yearning for Claudia's sake. She was always sad because we didn't have children, thinking she'd let me down somehow. That was crazy, of course, and I told her so. God knows we tried our damnedest."

He paused to finish the wine in his glass, and a look of deep sadness came over his face. "Anyway, now that it turns out I do have a family, the only problem is they don't know it. Probably never will. Ironic, isn't it?" He shook his head and she rose, then walked around the table and stood behind him. She folded her arms around his neck and kissed his cheek, very softly, then his lips. Taking his hand, she gently urged him to his feet.

A warm breeze from the south presaging the coming of spring fluttered the open louvers, making moonlight dance on the walls. His inner clock still registering west coast time, Phillip lay wide awake and watched contentedly. The roller coaster ride was over. The events of the past few days receded like the tide, sweeping out to sea the raw emotions that had clawed at him so unrelentingly. Here was peace. Here, in the arms of the woman he loved, in the bed that always held the scent of lavender. Here was his home and his haven, and here dwelt the keeper of his heart.

25

His immediate thought when the phone awakened him shortly after dawn this May morning was that Karla was calling from South Bend. She'd gone there to console June, who was having a hard time coping with the breakup of a long-term love affair. Her heart was broken, her self-esteem shattered, and she was in need of face-to-face sisterly comfort and reassurance. Phillip had no problem with not being invited on the journey. Best for them to have private time together without an extraneous man on the scene.

But it wasn't Karla on the other end this morning, it was Maddie sounding very unlike her usual upbeat self. Since leaving at the end of March she had phoned twice, reiterating her thanks for his having flown out to spend time with her mother. Each time Phillip had noticed a hesitancy when he asked how Amanda was doing, and now a somber note in her voice made his stomach tighten as he waited for her next words after exchanging greetings.

"Phillip, please forgive me for calling so early. I couldn't sleep and for some reason it was you I needed to talk to. I have really bad news and I don't know how to sugarcoat it." There it was. "I found out just hours ago how desperately ill my mother really is."

"Maddie, believe me when I tell you I am honored and grateful to be that person you had to call. But such terrible news! I'm so very sorry, my dear. I kind of thought something might be going on, last few times we talked. It was more what you weren't saying."

"You're very perceptive. I've been especially worried these last few months. You remember my telling you about her being thin, and of course you must have noticed it when you saw her. Well, it wasn't just grieving that made her lose interest in food, which is what I thought at first. It was part of it, I'm sure, but…she has cancer, a bad kind. Phillip, my Mom has cancer!" Her voice broke, and she started to cry.

The longing to be there, to hold her in his arms and comfort her, was so overwhelming all he could do was sit up and stare wordlessly at the stripe of early sunlight making its appearance through the flawed louver. It took a long moment before he could speak.

"Oh, Maddie. Dear Maddie, how awful for you, knowing how close you are with your mother. Can I ask how long you've suspected something was wrong? Not that it's any of my business…"

"But it is, Phillip. I could see when you were here there is still something, maybe a feeling of remembered fondness, between the two of you, no matter what happened such a long time ago." Her voice was strained but under control. "I just know you still care about what happens to each other, I could see that when I picked both of you up for dinner after you had time to talk. Anyway, I started to suspect something was wrong last summer but I had to be careful not to pry too much because she is a very private person. So I just kind of casually asked her if she'd had a checkup lately and she said 'Oh, last year, I guess, maybe a little longer ago. I'm fine, it's just that I get tired more often than I used to, but then I'm not getting any younger.' Well, true enough, nobody is, but it turned out that it had been more than just a little longer ago since that last checkup she mentioned."

"I completely understand why you were so worried. You probably thought besides grieving, there's this thing she told you about at lunch that day. I can see why you thought it might help her resolve that issue at least by looking me up and asking me to talk to her in person. But now I'm hearing that you had yet another concern, this one about her physical condition."

"I did, but I didn't pursue it. I was concentrating more on the guilt she was carrying. You'll never know how much nerve it took for me to look you up and ask for your help, Phillip. I took a risk, not knowing how you'd react to my proposal. But I'm so glad I went ahead and just did it."

"So am I. Because of course you're right that at some level we'll always care about what happens to each other. Thanks to your willingness to take a risk, we had a chance to talk face to face, something I never would have thought could happen, not in a million years. It enabled me to better understand certain things that happened in the past." Immediately he regretted having said even that much. Careful, Phillip, he cautioned himself, you're treading on extremely thin ice here. Fortunately, she didn't seem interested in pursuing what he'd just said and returned to concentrating on Amanda's current situation.

"I'm not exactly sure about the chronology, but anyway, I just found out that she has one of the worst, fastest developing of all cancers. Pancreatic. By the time it's diagnosed, there isn't much they can do and she said she doesn't want to go through all that terrible stuff like radiation and chemotherapy because it probably wouldn't work in the end anyway and oh, Phillip, I don't know how I can face the fact that it's terminal! Terminal!" here she broke down again, this time in sobs that broke his heart. He waited a few minutes to let her regain control before he spoke again.

"Maddie, my dear, is there anything I can do, anything at all? I know she has you and Melissa and your brothers and their families for support, but if there is any way that I can be of the smallest bit of help…"

"No, Phillip, honestly, there isn't." She blew her nose and her voice sounded hollow, like an echo from an empty well. "You did a wonderful thing coming here to talk to her. As horrible as this thing is that she's going through, she seems to have found a new kind of peace and I know a good part of it has to do with your coming to see her. Nobody could miss the change in her. Not Melissa, not even my brothers, busy as they are. I told them about your visit and how it came about, not in great detail of course. Just sketchily, but they seemed to get it."

She reassured him there was nothing he could do by coming back out, and the conversation ended with her promise to keep him informed. He sat still for a while after hanging up, reflecting on the all-too-swift passage of time and the brevity of mortal existence. Claudia's life was over and now it appeared inevitable that Amanda was facing the end of hers.

Karla was sitting beside him when Maddie called a month later. Amanda was gone, she said. She died peacefully with her family at her bedside. Her final weeks had been spent in hospice care and she was lucid until two days before the end. She had specified her wish for cremation in her will, the same request her husband had specified in his.

"I'm sorry to have to make this call, Phillip, but I promised to let you know. She suffered so much and her condition deteriorated faster than any of us expected, which the doctors said isn't unusual for this particular cancer. Anyway, as hard as it was to lose her, we had to take comfort knowing she was finally at peace, not suffering any longer. And with my Dad."

When Phillip hung up and repeated her words, Karla was silent for a moment, looking sad. Then she put her arm around him and said "It doesn't sound as though her mother told her, does it?"

"No it does not. And I have come to a decision, finally, about that. I will never tell her either."

How was it possible, he wondered later, that the events of less than one year in his youth could have haunted him all this time? Yet they had, perhaps because the impact of falling so deeply in love for the first time was so powerful. Then there was this: the pieces of the puzzle labeled Amanda never had been put together and something in his makeup would not allow him to let it go unsolved. Yes, that was it. But he'd finally gotten the answer while she was still alive, thank God. And in the process had received a gift, however bittersweet.

26

He did not anticipate hearing from Maddie so soon after she called to tell him Amanda had died; in fact, he doubted he'd hear from her in the near future, now that he'd completed his part in her effort to help her mother. True, she had talked about feeling a connection to him and expressed a desire to come back from to time, but he knew people sometimes said things in the moment that didn't necessarily stand the test of time. But here she was, calling him in the middle of a hot August morning, catching him as he returned from an early walk.

"Phillip? It's Maddie and I'm at the airport in Tampa. I just flew in on the red-eye." She paused to catch her breath. "I know I should have called before I got on the plane, but this hit me like lightning, this feeling that I had to see you. I just took a chance you'd be there. We need to get together face to face for a very private talk. I'm on my way to pick up a car and should be there soon, if that's okay with you."

"Of course it is. I'll be waiting for you. Drive carefully." He added the admonition because she sounded so upset.

When she pulled up in the driveway he was waiting for her in the small front garden, busying himself with plucking dead blossoms from the hibiscus bush. He walked quickly to open the door but she was already out, reaching for a bag on the front seat. He moved to take the bag but she held on to it as she greeted him and he stood there awkwardly, arms poised to hug her. Instead she leaned in to kiss him hurriedly on his cheek, then turned to close the car door.

"Inside," she said, surrendering the bag, "we need to go inside."

"Okay, Maddie," he said when they were seated facing each other in the living room, the bag at her feet, "now I hope you can let me in on the reason for this sudden visit and the air of mystery you've brought with you. Are you all right? Is Melissa all right?" He was about to say more but she cut him off, waving her hand impatiently.

"She's fine. I'm not. How can I possibly be all right, Phillip! Not when I don't have the faintest clue how I should feel, much less act in the presence of my biological father, damn it!" And she burst into tears.

"Oh My God." It was all he could say and he made himself sit still, waiting. She didn't speak again until she stopped crying, dug a tissue out of her purse and dried her eyes.

"Do you have any coffee? I had some on the plane but I have to have some right now!"

Glad to have something to do, he rose without speaking and headed for the kitchen. He was measuring coffee with trembling hands and jumped when she spoke behind him.

"Phillip. I'm sorry. I didn't intend to just blurt it out like that, it just came out. I kept rehearsing and rehearsing all the way here on the plane and way before that, as soon as I made up my mind I had to come here and talk to you about it."

"I'm glad you made that decision, Maddie. I feel just like you. I don't know what to feel or say or do either but now that you know, we absolutely need to talk about it. And it has to be face to face, so it's good you've come." He started the coffee maker, shaking his head. "She obviously told you I knew. I just didn't think she'd ever tell you. The story, I mean."

For a few minutes they stood in the kitchen studying each other in silence. Then Phillip gently guided her into the living room.

"You didn't see my home when you were here before, other than the living room." He was starting to feel better, in command. "You must want to freshen up after that all-night flight, so I'll let you find one of the bathrooms while I make breakfast for both of us. I'm hungry, and those red-eyes don't give you much of a breakfast, so what we are going to do now is sit down together and dive into an Ashcroft special.

Go."

He called Karla as he took the carton of eggs out of the refrigerator and gave her a quick rundown of what had just transpired. He hadn't had time to call her until now because the unexpected suddenness of Maddie's call had spurred him into action, making sure everything was in order, putting fresh hand towels in both bathrooms and generally tidying up, as his mother used to say.

Maddie reappeared, looking fresh and incredibly young.

"I wasn't even thinking about food, but oh those smells coming from this kitchen! I'm suddenly downright famished. Can I help?"

"Yes, by seating yourself at the table and being patient while I whip this thing up." It dawned on him that he was standing here making breakfast for his daughter. The thought struck him as surprisingly natural and made him smile.

A little later they were sitting in the living room with mugs of coffee and a coffee cake he'd taken from the freezer and warmed in the microwave. Helping herself to a slice, Maddie sighed contentedly.

"The one and only time I was here before, you fed me leftovers. I was nervous and I felt suddenly hungry when you asked me if I'd had dinner. I said I hadn't and you made me, a stranger, feel right at home somehow. Remember?" He nodded. Would he ever forget that first encounter?

"So I guess in a way I associate you with food, which in my book equals comfort. And that's what I feel when I'm with you, Phillip. Comfortable. I'm not even nervous right now. How is that possible, with what we both know?"

"God only knows. I was sure as hell shaking in my boots when you told me you knew, and that you knew I knew. I should have guessed what it was when you called me so unexpectedly this morning. Must be getting dense up here." He tapped a forefinger against his forehead.

She shook her head. "No," she said, taking a sip of coffee, "My Mom said she gave you permission to tell me, so probably you didn't think she'd be the one to do it. Out of curiosity, Phillip, do you think you ever would have told me?"

"I have always believed you should never say never, because time and circumstance change so many things in life. But in this case, I never would have told you. She said she hadn't, because after losing your father she did not want to throw something like that at you .Well,

I felt the same way. I did not see a reason to disturb such a major element in the foundation of your life."

"Phillip, do you have any idea how what you just said strikes me? I can't believe anyone could be that unselfish." He didn't know what to say in response, and after a moment she continued.

"What I mean is, you told me how much you and Claudia wanted children but were unable to have them. Then after I talked you into going to L.A. with me, you found out you really did have a child. Me. You never had a chance to see me or get to know me, through no fault of your own. And because I have a daughter myself, I can only imagine how deeply that had to cut. Yet my mother gave you the go-ahead to let me know I was your daughter, and you're telling me you decided you never would have, out of consideration for me. That makes you my hero, Phillip."

"I'm no hero, Maddie. And I'm not being modest saying that. What happened in the past, I figured, was exactly that. The past. I thanked Amanda for telling me about you. It was a gift, something I never in a million years could have anticipated, knowing that I was a father. That was more than enough for me. I felt a strong connection with you before I knew you were my daughter, and as I recall, you said pretty much the same thing. I was content with your telling me we would see each other again. I held on to that hope. What threw me for a loop was your coming here today with the news that she had told you."

"She was close to the end when it happened. She said it was something she had to do while she was still able, let me know the truth and trust me to do with it whatever I felt was right. I loved my mother so much, Phillip, and loved her even more for telling me. It had to cost her a lot, but as sick and as near death as she was, she summoned up the courage to do what she felt she had to. She knew you so well, and knew you wouldn't do it. Now what we do with it is up to us, isn't it? Any thoughts?"

He pondered for a moment. "So far I think we're doing okay with it. You just said you were comfortable and I feel the same. For now I guess I'd have to say we don't have to actually do anything. Perhaps just let the discovery sink in and see what part it might play in the future."

"That's well put. No drama, I gather, is what you're saying. The universe does seem to have remained in balance despite what we both know. I will venture one thought, and that is for now it might be best to keep it between us. Other than your lady, Karla, who I'm guessing you've told."

He nodded. "We have no secrets, Karla and I. We've pretty much told each other about most of the meaningful things that have gone on in our lives. We have a common bond where childlessness is concerned, although our stories are different. When I told her about you, she was so shocked she let go of the glass that held the martini I'd made for her. After I cleaned up the mess and made her another one, she recovered and was thrilled for me." He smiled, remembering, and said "I know she'll be very eager to see you."

"To be honest, Phillip, I didn't know exactly how this visit would go, so I bought a ticket with an open return. I was uncertain about how long I'd stay."

"Well, now that we've gotten past the initial meeting of minds on this, Maddie, I hope you won't leave right away. I mean, I think it would be good for both of us to spend some time getting used to knowing what we know and knowing each of us knows the other one...oh, for God's sake, I'm babbling. Forgive me."

"That's okay, Phillip, you're entitled, we both are, to act a little off balance. This is a big, big discovery after all."

"You're very kind, you know. But let's get down to making a plan for now. I have a perfectly comfortable guest room ready and waiting for you, and I would love to have you spend at least a couple of days here. Unless you have pressing business at home, that is."

She thought for a few minutes before accepting "Okay, thanks, if you're sure it isn't an imposition. I mean, I really arrived with no warning. I've been thinking about it for such a long time, should I call, should I ask if I could come, and finally it was just do it before you lose your nerve. Just get on a plane and pop in. You have to have this conversation with him."

"Imposition? You're not serious. You? No, it would make me very happy if we could spend some time together. We have a lot to talk about, after all."

"That's very sweet of you. I'll accept your nice invitation. But then I will have to get back because I do have some pressing business at home. Work, and also loose ends still waiting to be tied up with .Mom's estate, the house and all that stuff. My brothers are doing a lot but they're very busy with their own obligations."

Karla asked them to dinner that first night, an invitation that was quickly accepted. Maddie was especially eager to see her place after hearing Phillip's description of the view, which she found enthralling. A fresh breeze had blown in from the Gulf after a spectacular sunset, and they ate on the lanai. Karla had served Key West shrimp sautéed in lemon butter and garlic, which Maddie said was one of her all-time favorite dinners. After eating every morsel of a generous slice of fresh Key lime pie, she pronounced it a perfect Florida meal and told Karla she would have come all the way from L.A. just for the delicious food and wonderful evening she'd so graciously provided.

They were home shortly before ten, and Maddie remarked that it was still early for her.

"In case you're thinking I'm tired," she said as they walked in the door, "I'm really not. We're going to stay up a while, you and I, because I have something very special for you in my bag. Did you notice it was heavy for its size when you carried it inside this morning?"

"I did, now that you mention it. I must tell you, though, on the way back just now I was thinking you had to be exhausted after that all-night flight and our long walk on the beach this afternoon. And then I remembered how young and therefore how resilient you must be. So okay, I'm ready for whatever you've brought me."

She went into the guest room and reappeared with a large photo album. No wonder the bag was so heavy, this thing was huge! They sat close together on the sofa and began the first of several hours of looking at the pictures. She told him that before Amanda went into hospice, but after deciding she would tell Maddie the truth about her heritage, she started on this project. She must have spent days carefully selecting and arranging pictures so that should her daughter decide to tell him she knew he was her biological father, she could present him with a photographic history of herself from the day she was born all throughout her life until recent years. She sat close beside him, offering pertinent facts and humorous observations about what was happening when each photograph was taken. His eyes lingered on the picture taken at the hospital when she was a newborn. He could hardly stop gazing at the tiny face which was all that showed above the pink bunting.

"And that cute little pink knitted cap" she said, pointing, "hid my hair. I was not bald like a lot of babies are. My Mom said I had a good crop of curly red hair. Like you had, Phillip, when you were young. I found that out, of course when she told me you were my biological father. But when I was growing up and someone would comment on my being the only redhead in the family she'd say it must have been a gene passed down from the Stewarts, who were originally from Scotland."

"Yes, I was a redhead as far back as I can remember. Got it from my Dad's side of the family. Stayed red till it took a notion to turn gray. Or silver, which my lady barber back home in Michigan called it, and vain old guy that I am, I like it better."

She looked at him, studying his hair. "She was right. I know the difference. I would call it silver, and you have a lot of it. You're lucky."

"Thank you. I would call it being genetically blessed."

The album lay across both their laps, forgotten for the moment as a thoughtful look crossed her face. "You know," she said slowly, "I looked different all my life from my brothers. Being the only girl, I don't think anyone really gave it a thought. The boys looked a lot like Dad, although they had her deep blue eyes and his were brown. They're two years apart and people always took them for twins. Dana, the younger one, is taller than Daniel, which made them look the same age when they were growing up. Both have dark brown, almost black hair like my Dad and both started losing their hair in their early forties, which was when my Dad started losing his. They still look handsome and are far from bald, but their hair is definitely looking thinner and kind of receding at the forehead. I remember being in high school when my friends and I were really into showing off our hair. I was the only redhead, and by then it wasn't curly anymore, just a little wavy and I wore it long, mostly in a ponytail. So I got attention but my Mom had the kind of hair I always wanted. Hers was a beautiful chestnut color with lots of highlights in the sun, especially. It was gorgeous. You probably don't remember it, it was such a long time ago." Ah, but he did remember. Oh yes, he remembered that hair.

The photographs were mostly of Maddie alone, holding a cake or blowing out candles on each birthday; school plays; wearing

Halloween costumes; first days of school; dressed in Easter finery in front of a church, and sitting on the floor in front of a Christmas tree, opening gifts. There were family pictures, of course, some with her brothers, some with one or both parents. Graduation pictures, wedding pictures, holding a newborn Melissa. All there, carefully placed according to ages and stages, accompanied by detailed information in Amanda's handwriting which was a little shaky but clearly legible.

The last page featured pictures of a proud Maddie standing arm in arm with her daughter in cap and gown at her high school graduation. His eyes filled and he looked at her as he closed the album.

"There are no words to tell you what this means to me, Maddie. I can see this is her final, incredible gift to me. And she was so sick. It's truly a labor of love." His voice cracked on the last three words, and his eyes were moist.

"Yes, it is, and I know she did it out of love for both of us. It's yours to keep, of course. This is her handiwork. I made copies of all the pictures and put them in a separate album for Melissa to have someday. My Mom was a very organized person, as you might know."

He did know. He remembered helping her that morning in East Lansing with the boxes she was sending home. Her orderliness had made the task easy, and he'd told her how much he appreciated it. Now he had before him a priceless keepsake and final reminder of that special quality of hers.

Karla bowed out of joining them for a last dinner, using an excuse so transparent Phillip was amused. He knew her so well, knew she wanted them to have every moment to themselves exclusively. Maddie had slept in that morning, finally giving in to the effects of jet lag. He took advantage of the opportunity to buy a bottle of champagne at his favorite wine shop, a prized vintage Louis Roederer that cost so much it made what he paid for the Moet he bought for his and Amanda's last night in East Lansing look like chicken feed by comparison. When she woke up they had juice and coffee and fresh croissants he'd picked up at the new French bakery next to the wine shop. She wanted to walk with him, waving off his protests that he couldn't keep up with her.

"I know how you walk, my dear Maddie. I watched you often enough. I think they call it speed walking, and these old knees are no match for that pace. Why don't you go ahead, and I'll plod along behind you."

"That's ridiculous, and you know it. I don't do real speed walking, and you're no slouch when it comes to maintaining a pace I would rate as far above average. And not just for your age. I watched you too, remember? Now come on and we can have a good time talking while we walk. I'll be on the plane to L.A at this time tomorrow, so let's get going. And when we get back I demand another Ashcroft special for breakfast."

The rest of the day sped by, and she insisted on dinner at Salty Sam's. She wanted fish fresh from the Gulf, she said, and she knew from having lived here that was the place that never failed to disappoint. He'd wanted to take her to a fine seafood restaurant on the Key, a new one that had earned excellent reviews, but he had to give in when she pointed out that this was familiar territory and that the whole visit was a special kind of homecoming.

They stayed up late talking and looking through the album again. He knew he would feast on those photographs, that he would study each one over and over with never-ending interest.

"What about you, Phillip? I'm sure you have pictures of your family, and I'd love to see them. Especially your parents, my biological grandparents."

"I have a couple of albums that Claudia put together. I'll get them."

They spent an hour or so looking at photographs of Phillip's family and the house in which he'd grown up

"I'd like some copies of these if you wouldn't mind sending them to me. I would keep them just for personal reasons, to take out whenever I get the urge to look at pictures of people I never knew but with whom I share a bond of heredity. Do you know what I mean?"

"I do indeed. The first time I ever saw you, something about your eyes intrigued me, rang a bell if you will. Later I realized you had inherited my mother's eyes, the color and the shape. My father always loved her eyes and called them mysterious cat eyes."

"That's very romantic and interesting. I think I can see it in some of these pictures. As I said, my eyes were neither my Mom's beautiful deep blue nor my Dad's brown, and now I know where they came from. I'm glad Mom wanted me to know about you being my biological father, Phillip, and now that I do, it hasn't shaken the foundation of my life as you feared. Yes, she was wise not to tell me soon after my Dad died because it would have inflicted an awful blow, missing him as much as I did. I always will miss him dreadfully, but time has a way of healing wounds, and I was ready to hear what she told me when the time came. But I want that knowledge to end with the two of us and of course Karla. I see no reason to tell my daughter or my brothers because it really is of no concern to them and would only stir up God knows what kinds of speculations and perceptions about who she was and what she did when she was a young woman in college. Do you agree?"

"I could not agree more, Maddie. It's a closed book."

"Of course Brett will always be my only father, the one I've known since I was born. But now that I've met you and have gotten to know you and the kind of person you are, Phillip, I have plenty of room in my heart and mind for you. My Mom knew what she was doing when she told me you are my biological father. She knew you would not tell me, which makes you my hero, as I've said. I promise you we will never lose contact with each other, if I have anything to say about it."

"Same goes for me, Maddie. You can't possibly know how happy I am to hear you say that."

"I think we're doing great so far, don't you? I was so, I don't know, uncertain about how this would go. I mean coming here with no warning and having this face to face meeting…you have to agree it's pretty out of the ordinary, our situation. And kind of weird."

"Weird, no. Out of the ordinary, yes. In fact I would call it extraordinary because that has much nicer, almost magical implications. And I agree, we are doing great. Really great, Maddie."

"One last thing. Now that I know all about you and who you really are, it occurs to me that I am not an orphan. Technically speaking."

"You're right. Yes, by God, you're absolutely right."

It was time to break out the champagne he'd placed in the refrigerator hours before. He held it up triumphantly.

"Oh my God, Phillip!" She stared at the label. "What did you do, win the lottery?"

"You could say that, yes." He nodded, smiling as he uncorked the bottle. "I won the big one. The jackpot. My prize? Finding out I have a daughter, an absolutely beautiful, amazing daughter."

27

"I know it sounds crazy but I tell you I can feel it. In my bones! We are going to see the green flash this very evening!" Karla licked the last bit of chocolate frosting from her fingers and set the plate that had held the brownies inside the wicker basket. Then she closed it and held her glass for Phillip to pour more champagne. Noting that his glass was almost empty, she looked at the bottle and asked "A little more for you? There's plenty left." He smiled, shaking his head and said "I'm the driver, remember?" With that, he touched his glass to hers and said "Happy anniversary, darling."

"Happy anniversary. One year exactly since we met. I remembered the date of my party, but how did you remember?"

"I'll answer by saying how could I forget? Besides, I hung on to your invitation, sentimental me."

They were at the beach, their lounge chairs facing the Gulf. Phillip had suggested a sunset picnic dinner and Karla thought it was an excellent idea, offering to make her special frosted double chocolate brownies.

Now, he was thinking, if we see the green flash it will be a perfect ending to a perfect day that had begun with a long phone conversation with Maddie. She had called a couple of times since returning to Los Angeles to check in, as she put it, on her sole remaining parent. The thought and the sound of her voice brought a smile to Phillip's lips and a warmth to that special place she'd made for herself in his heart. Later there was that encounter with Art, whom he hadn't seen since Thanksgiving. He'd gone to Tia Lena's to pick up the Cuban sandwiches for their picnic and there was Art, working behind the counter and smiling when he saw Phillip walk in the door. Best of all, he looked healthy and clean, and the smart white hat looked good atop neatly cut hair. He told Phillip he had a counselor he liked a lot who had helped him find a studio apartment within walking distance of the restaurant. He hesitated before handing the bag to Phillip, and leaned forward, motioning him to come closer.

"The best thing, Mr. Phillip sir, is I have a girlfriend, a really nice young lady. Don't look over right now but that's her at the cash register. She's teaching me Spanish and I'm catching on pretty fast," he said proudly. "It took me a while after I talked to you at Thanksgiving, but then one day it hit me that you were talking plain old common sense. I went back for help at that social services place and I got it. Went into rehab again and now I been here since right after Christmas and Lena just gave me a raise." He held out his hand and Phillip shook it. Then he paid for the sandwiches and left, giving Art a thumbs up out of sight of the pretty dark-haired cashier. Yes, a perfect day all around.

"You said you've seen it once, Phillip, and you never forgot it. Now it's my turn." Karla was sipping champagne and he finished the remainder in his glass. "Or I should say" she added, "our turn to see it together. And what could be better than seeing it on a day as special as this one!"

"Yes, it's unforgettable and yes, I want to see it again, with you. Hopefully more than once. It's quite a phenomenon. Conditions have to be just so, and it happens so fast you can't even blink. Let's see", he said, squinting, "watch the sun. Focus, focus. I'll hazard a guess that we're going to see it right…about…now."

It was there and gone in the blink of an eye. A lightning-quick flash of green just above the horizon, disappearing with the swiftness of a camera click. Karla let out the breath she had been holding. "Oh, I can't believe I saw it! I saw it!" She set her glass on the basket and clapped her hands. The sun had disappeared from view, swallowed by the Gulf, and in its afterglow the clouds were exploding with color, bright gold, fiery pink, in a sky still blue but deepening fast.

"I'd forgotten how magnificent it is," Phillip remarked. "We really should come to the beach more often. You never know when you might see another offering from Mother Nature's bag of magic tricks. I guess when you have it right in your back yard, you take it for granted."

"Magic tricks from Mother Nature. Why Phillip, that's downright poetic. What a lovely thought." She turned to look at him and Phillip's heart turned over. She had no idea, he thought, how beautiful she was right now, her face bare of makeup, the sudden breeze off the Gulf lifting her blonde hair into disarray in a way he found irresistible. Her blue eyes were alight with excitement. He couldn't help himself, he simply had to kiss those lips, unmindful of the few people who walked by, leaving the beach.

"I know something I could never take for granted" she said, "and that's the way you kiss me, like you just did. Never."

"Ready?" she asked, setting the glasses inside the basket, and starting to rise from her chair. He gripped her wrist and said "Not quite. Let's stay a little longer."

They sat quietly, holding hands and watching the colors fade into a sky rapidly turning purple. After a while Karla said "This reminds me of the night when I came back from South Bend and you told me you loved me. Remember?"

"Oh yes, I remember. I remember how hard it was for me to think of how to say it without sounding like an idiot, but you saved me when you didn't make me wait to hear you say that you were in love with me." He tightened his grip on her hand.

"Well, I was. I am now, but so much more. Phillip, you're everything I ever wanted in a man, you're…"

"Then marry me!" It shot out of his mouth and neither could speak for a long moment.

Karla recovered first. "Did you really just say the M word, Phillip? I thought you were content with the way things are with us."

"Of course I am. You're my lover. My best friend. You opened a door to a new life for me, a door I thought was closed for good."

"Then why change things? And why now?"

He tilted his head up. The half-moon, faint just moments ago, was brightening rapidly and stars were beginning to multiply across the almost completely black sky. He released her hand and laced his fingers together.

"Karla, forgive me. I should never have blurted it out like that. I probably scared the hell out of you."

"No, Phillip, no. I didn't mean to sound as if you scared me. I only wanted to know why. It just came out of the blue, and yes, it was kind of a jolt."

"I didn't want it to come out that way," he said in a low voice. "Truth is, I've been thinking about it for a long time but somehow I couldn't find the moment I was waiting for. Right now just hit me as a perfect time for a possible miracle so I thought I'd grab the opportunity. But I get the impression the idea doesn't appeal to you. Let's forget I said it."

"Oh, no you don't!" She reached to unclasp his hands, holding both of them in her own. "Who said it doesn't appeal to me? You have to give me a minute or two to recover from the shock. It isn't every day I get proposed to, you know. But I'm asking you to simply tell me why you want to marry me."

"Why? Because I love you, Karla, that's why. How's that for simplicity?"

"Yes, I know, and I love you too, but that still isn't an answer, Phillip. You have me without all the legalities. It isn't as though we're kids. And we could live together, which we practically do right now, without getting married. It's happening much more often than in former times, as I'm sure you've observed, and especially with older couples. I know quite a few, here and back home. In some cases there are things like financial considerations that make marriage impractical."

"I don't think either of us gives a damn about that. I don't, anyway. Do you?"

"Heavens, no. Neither of us has to worry about security where money is concerned. Now answer my question."

"All right," he sighed, "I'll see what I can do with words then, but I'm not good at that kind of thing."

"Yes you are, Phillip. You say only what you mean, and that's very important to me. I love the way you talk, so get over yourself."

"Okay, here goes." He cleared his throat. "I want to marry you, my darling, because I believe in the institution of marriage. It is a good, solid, old-fashioned tradition. I want to be your husband, and I would be honored to have you for my wife. We keep hearing these days about how a piece of paper doesn't really mean much or change things, especially with older people, but I value that piece of paper as undeniable proof of a sacred covenant between two people who have vowed to live out their lives together. Of course, at the same time I'm also completely aware of the difference in our ages…"

"Which as I have told you, is so meaningless, it is of absolutely no consequence and does not deserve even a mention. My God, Phillip, we could have a lot of very good years ahead of us, loving each other, being happy, traveling, seeing new places together. You of all people should know the only certainty in life is that there is no certainty. Who has a crystal ball? I don't, and I wouldn't want one. You have to go for it. So if you have a chance at happiness, why wouldn't you grab it?" The words had rushed out in a torrent, and she paused for breath.

He was confused. "Karla, what are you saying? Maybe I'm too dense to interpret it, but…"

"Yes! I'm saying yes!" She shouted it so loudly a gull pecking at crumbs nearby flew off with a great flutter of wings. "Yes, Phillip, I'll marry you! Whenever you want, the sooner the better. I want to be your wife for as long as we both shall live, in sickness and in health and all the rest of it. I just wanted to hear you say why you want to marry me so I could be sure that you're sure that…oh, you've got me so flustered I don't even know what I'm saying." She stood, pulled him to his feet, and wound her arms around his waist, tight enough to make him gasp a little, which pleased her. Then she kissed him.

Lugging the chairs, basket and small cooler made it challenging to walk with their arms around each other, but somehow they managed. They climbed the few steps to the boardwalk, then stopped for a last look at the Gulf, clearly visible now in the moonlight. Setting down their paraphernalia, they stood listening for a little while to the pulsating music of the surf, not speaking, reflecting on the enormity of what had just happened. Finally, it was Karla who broke the silence.

"The green flash," she said softly. "It was worth waiting for."

Made in the USA
Columbia, SC
03 November 2018